FINDING
FORTUNE

FINDING FORTUNE

Pippa Goodhart

Catnip

CATNIP BOOKS
Published by Catnip Publishing Ltd
320 City Road
London EC1V 2NZ

This edition published 2013
3 5 7 9 10 8 6 4 2

Text copyright © 2013 Pippa Goodhart
Inside map illustrations copyright © 2013 Michael Goodhart
Cover map 'Going to Klondyke' by May Bloom, published 1897, is in the
collection of the Geography & Map Division

The moral rights of the author and illustrator have been asserted.

A CIP catalogue record for this book is available from the British Library.

ISBN 978-1-84647-159-9

Printed in India

www.catnippublishing.co.uk

*For Tom Deveson who gave
me the gift of a free choice of book
forty-three years ago, and helped
turn me into a reader*

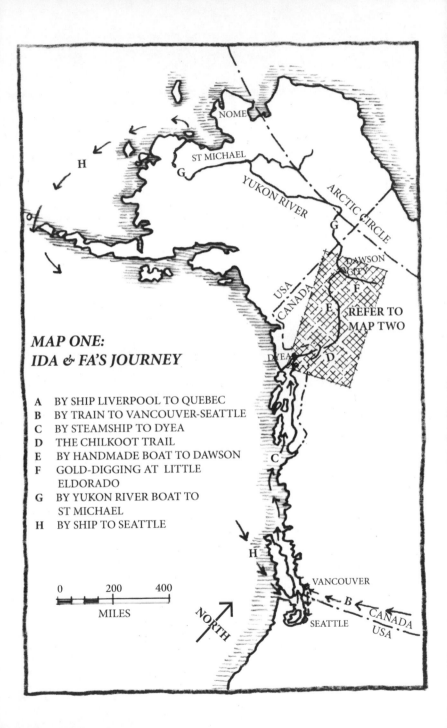

MAP ONE:
IDA & FA'S JOURNEY

A   BY SHIP LIVERPOOL TO QUEBEC
B   BY TRAIN TO VANCOUVER-SEATTLE
C   BY STEAMSHIP TO DYEA
D   THE CHILKOOT TRAIL
E   BY HANDMADE BOAT TO DAWSON
F   GOLD-DIGGING AT LITTLE
    ELDORADO
G   BY YUKON RIVER BOAT TO
    ST MICHAEL
H   BY SHIP TO SEATTLE

0   200   400
MILES

NORTH

NOME
ST MICHAEL
YUKON RIVER
ARCTIC CIRCLE
DAWSON CITY
USA
CANADA
REFER TO
MAP TWO
DYEA
VANCOUVER
CANADA
USA
SEATTLE

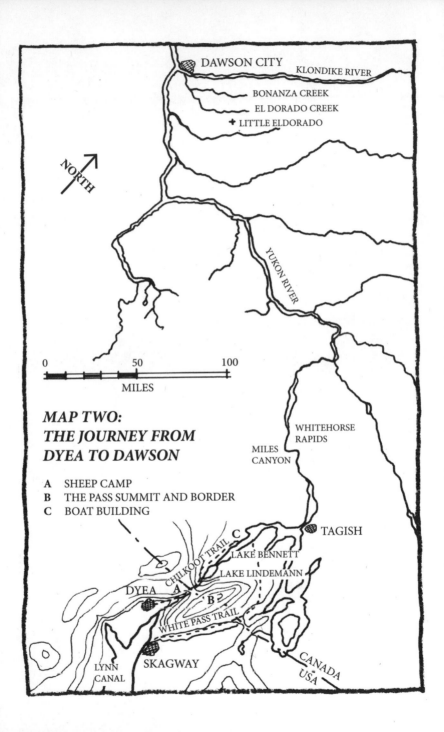

KLONDIKE RIVER

DAWSON CITY

BONANZA CREEK

EL DORADO CREEK

✝ LITTLE ELDORADO

NORTH

YUKON RIVER

0   50   100
MILES

WHITEHORSE
RAPIDS

MILES
CANYON

MAP TWO:
THE JOURNEY FROM
DYEA TO DAWSON

A SHEEP CAMP
B THE PASS SUMMIT AND BORDER
C BOAT BUILDING

TAGISH

C

CHILKOOT TRAIL

LAKE BENNETT

LAKE LINDEMANN

DYEA   A

B

WHITE PASS TRAIL

SKAGWAY

LYNN
CANAL

CANADA
USA

1

Ida looked at the stone slab under her feet. She read the twirly writing that listed names and dates of her dead Berringer ancestors. Soon Mama's name would be added to that list.

Isabella Metcalf 1866–1897

Was Mama an 'ancestor' too, now that she was dead, wondered Ida? Ancestor didn't feel right for someone who hadn't been old and hadn't lived a very long time ago.

Last Friday they had lowered the coffin with Mama's body in it into the vault. The Berringer family – Grandmama, Uncle Stephen and Aunt Helen, their three children, Aunt Theodora, and some elderly cousins Ida didn't even know – had all been dressed in stiff, stifling outfits of sombre black to parade behind the coffin, out of the summer sunshine and into the church. The estate servants and people from the village had worn their best black too, shuffling and watching. Like crows, thought Ida.

She and Fa were there, holding hands very tightly, not quite belonging to either of the groups. Grandmama had insisted that she, Lady Berringer, was principle mourner, following directly behind the coffin. So, in death, the Berringer family had reclaimed their Isabella and pushed Fa and Ida to one side.

Now Ida's eyes welled with hot tears. She blinked hard and wiped the back of her hand crossly over her face as she ran, clattering her feet, down the aisle and out of the church. She ran out into sunshine and air that was fresh. Ida hitched up her long black skirts and began to climb an old apple tree that drooped a branch down as if to invite her up. She went up into the tree's branches, then leaned against the trunk and looked out through a dancing veil of leaves. When I die, thought Ida, I want a grave outside in the sunshine.

Of course, it was proper that Mama had been put in the family grave. Mama was a Berringer, even though her family had hardly spoken to her after she married Fa and became a Metcalf. Fa was not 'one of us', according to Grandmama. He was not of their social class. So that made Ida only half 'one of us'. Which half, she wondered?

The hustle-rustle of leaves in the breeze all around brought to Ida's mind the sounds of the sea at home, in Norfolk. Fa and Mama and Ida had lived there in a small damp house with knapped flints pressed into its walls. Behind the house were dunes of sand and scratchy grass, then a beach of millions upon millions of pebbles, each one of them different in size and colour and shape. The pebble beach sloped steeply down to a great green-grey sea that was never still. The sea was pulled and pushed by the tides, rolling and tossing and rattling the pebbles as it sucked them in and spat them out, then it sighed a froth of foam as it stroked the last lick of each wave over them.

They had been happy in Norfolk until Mama had got sick, coughing and thin and pale.

'Is it any surprise that she is ill?' said Grandmama's letters, 'living in that hovel of a home?'

Fa and Ida had cooked Mama tasty broths to try and make her strong. They had kept Mama warm and made her laugh, but she continued getting worse until the day came when she coughed spots of blood onto her white lace handkerchief. Then Fa had come downstairs from Mama's room with his face as white as milk.

'Is it very bad?' Ida had asked. And Fa had looked at Ida and nodded.

'Isabella must be brought here and cared for properly,' was Grandmama's response when told. She had sent her carriage to fetch Mama, along with Fa and Ida.

So they had left Norfolk and gone to live in the Dower House, near the main gate of the Berringer family estate of Yewdale Hall. Grandmama had loaned them Tilly, an undermaid, as well as a cook to help care for Mama. She had also sent her own doctor.

Grandmama had visited poor sick Mama, curling her lip when she saw the way that Fa had taken over the parlour for his painting because the light was best in that room.

'I shall see Isabella in her rest room,' Grandmama

would say. She could never bring herself to say 'bedroom'. She would sweep into the room where Mama lay propped up on pillows in her bed. Fa would make tea and send Ida up with a tray laid with the best china and with a vase of flowers freshly picked from the garden.

They all did anything they could think of to make Mama well. Fa hardly slept at all by the end, constantly sitting at Mama's side in case she needed anything. Ida read Mama storybooks, especially adventure stories by G.A. Henty that her cousin Eric lent them. Those stories were full of unladylike things such as shooting and bad language, but Mama didn't mind. When Ida noticed Mama wince with pain she would hesitate in her reading, but Mama would always smile and say, 'Go on. The story takes my mind off the discomfort.' So Ida read lots, taking Mama and herself to countries and times far away from real life in the Dower House.

But, in spite of their care, Mama died; now she was in the Berringer tomb for ever.

Ida closed her eyes and let the tree rock her. 'But I am Ida Adelaide Metcalf,' she told the tree. 'I am not a Berringer.'

With one arm secure around a branch, Ida pulled the ribbon from her plaited hair and shook it free. She undid the top button on her high-necked black bodice. She wished that she could kick off the tightly buttoned boots and strip down her stockings so that her legs could be free, as they so often were in Norfolk.

They would be serving tea in the big house now and Ida should be there. She would be scolded for being late.

'Well, let them be cross!' She couldn't think properly with the cousins and their nanny watching every move and insisting on 'polite conversation'.

In Norfolk, Fa would serve the tea beside the little cast iron fireplace in the small front room. Mama would sip from her cup, the saucer held elegantly in the other hand. Then she would laugh as she tried biting into one of the hard little rock cakes that Fa had cooked.

'Dip them into the tea. That makes them softer,' Ida advised Mama. But Mama would never do anything so unladylike. She nibbled at her dry rock cake. Ida dunked her own, making it soggy enough to collapse all down her pinafore.

Fa laughed.

'You two are incorrigible!' smiled Mama.

'I want to go home,' Ida told the tree. She jumped down and ran towards the Dower House to find Fa.

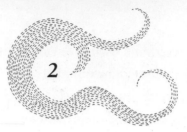

2

Ida ran through the estate's park of ancient oak trees and grass and grazing sheep towards the Dower House. She ran up the path, past rose beds, and in through the open door.

'Fa!' shouted Ida. 'Fa?'

There was no reply. But there were voices upstairs. Not Fa's voice, but the shrill voice of Aunt Dora. Why might she be here? Aunt Dora had hardly visited when Mama was alive, and certainly hadn't been here since Mama's death.

Ida froze statue-still to listen from the hallway as Aunt Dora said, 'You see, Mr Smollet, my brother-in-law Frank is up in town about some business today, so this is an opportunity to assess the house for the improvements my mother, Lady Berringer, has proposed.'

Ida frowned. Improvements? Maybe Grandmama was instructing that Mr Smollet should install gas lighting to replace the candles? Mr Smollet was a builder, so it must be something of that kind. How strange of Grandmama to turn generous just now. But how rude to send people into their home without even asking permission! And how awful if Grandmama went to all the trouble and expense of improving the Dower House, only to be told that Ida and Fa were going home to Norfolk!

Ida slipped back out into the garden. So, Fa was in town. Why might that be? Why hadn't he told her? They are all of them keeping secrets from me, thought Ida! Well, I shall go and ask Grandmama directly what she is about and warn her that Fa and I are about to go home.

Ida marched up the rhododendron-bordered drive towards the 'big house', meeting Tilly round a corner.

'Oh, there you are, Miss Ida!' Tilly's kind face was pink from hurrying. 'Nanny said that you weren't at nursery tea. Wherever have you been, Miss?'

'I am sorry, Tilly,' said Ida. 'You see, I was going to the big house, but I stopped by at the church and . . .'

Tilly put a hand on Ida's arm. 'Oh, Miss Ida. You wanted to be with your mama. Of course you did.'

'Then I went to find Fa. He wasn't there, but Aunt Dora was, sneaking around with . . .'

'Well, your father is expected back soon and the two of you are to attend dinner with Lady Berringer this evening. So perhaps it is as well that you didn't eat your fill of nursery tea after all! Apparently Her Ladyship has some news that she wants to tell the two of you over dinner.'

'Oh dear,' said Ida. 'I think that I know what that news is. She's planning to make the Dower House nicer for Fa and me.'

'Is she now?' Tilly gave Ida a doubting kind of look. 'Whatever makes you suppose that, Miss?'

So Ida told her about the conversation between Aunt Dora and Mr Smollet as Tilly bustled her in through the back entrance of the big house and down the stairs to the servants' quarters.

'We must make you presentable,' said Tilly, glancing at the clock. 'There's no time to return to the Dower House for fresh clothes, especially if your aunt is there and hoping not to be disturbed. We must just make the best of what you have on.' Tilly looked at Ida. 'Button up that neck, Miss, if you please. Goodness, your hair is like a teasel! It's lucky that you are still in mourning. Nothing elaborate would be either expected or proper, but we must tidy you up. Take off your boots, Miss, and Timmy can give them a polish. I'll see what I can do with that hair, but first let's put that kettle on the hob. Cook is up to her eyes with your dinner to prepare, but I think she'll allow us a cup of tea.'

'Thank you, Tilly,' said Ida.

Tilly did what she could with Ida's hair and a broad black ribbon that she took from a drawer.

'Just like your mother's – full of curls!' said Tilly, tugging a brush through the tangles.

'Oh-ouch!'

'There! I think you'll do.'

As they sipped their tea, there was a sound of wheels

crunching on gravel outside the steps. Ida peeped out of the window, where the driveway was at eye level.

'It's a dog cart,' she said.

'That'll be your father arriving from the station,' said Tilly, tucking a strand of hair behind Ida's ear. 'Put those boots back on and straighten your skirts. You and your father can wait in the drawing room for the dinner gong to sound.'

Up in the hallway Fa stood tugging at his beard and looking awkward as Ida's cousins Charlotte and Elena danced around him.

'Did you get the position at the bank, Uncle Frank?' asked Charlotte.

'Uncle Frank will work in a bank!' giggled Elena.

'Except,' said Fa, blushing slightly, 'that Uncle Frank will not work in a bank. I was not appointed.'

'Fa?' said Ida, and Fa turned towards her.

'Ida! You and I are to dine with your Grandmama and the aunts.'

'That's what Tilly says,' said Ida.

Charlotte gave Ida a poke on the arm. 'Are you really? In the dining room? Is that why you weren't at tea? Nanny was cross, you know.'

Fa raised questioning eyebrows at Ida, but she stuck her chin upwards.

'I didn't want to spoil my appetite for the party that Grandmama is arranging for Fa and me.'

'Party!' shrieked Elena. 'Ooh, that is unfair! Why are we not invited?'

'Oh, are you not?' said Ida. 'Poor you.'

'I'm going to ask Mother!' said Elena, and she and Charlotte raced up the stairs, calling for their Mama.

Ida and Fa moved into the hushed drawing room full of chairs and sofas and curtains in dark colours. Fa perched awkwardly on the edge of a well-stuffed sofa. 'Do I look suitable?' he asked, easing the cravat at his neck.

Ida looked at tall skinny Fa with his mass of dark brown hair and beard and those big dark eyes peering anxiously out of his pale face. He was wearing his black funeral jacket and trousers, quite new, and his beard had been trimmed for Mama's funeral last week. But somehow, Fa could never look properly smart, not like Uncle Stephen who could always look plump and dashing in army dress uniform. Fa was 'all legs and arms, elbows and knees,' Mama used to say.

'You look nice,' Ida told him, and she squeezed his arm.

'What do you suppose this dinner is all about, eh?' asked Fa. 'Is it really some kind of a party? That seems unlikely.'

Ida shrugged. 'Tilly just said dinner, but that is a kind of party. I think that Grandmama wants to be nice to us.' Ida looked at Fa's furrowed brow and she wagged a finger at him as Mama had sometimes done. 'Why didn't you tell me that you were going to town? Tilly knew. Aunt Dora knew and even Charlotte and Elena knew, but not me! And what did they mean about a position in a bank?'

Fa raised his hands in a hopeless kind of gesture. 'I didn't tell you because I thought that I could perhaps surprise you with good news on my return. I went to speak to a gentleman about a possible position working in a large bank in Manchester.'

'But we don't want to be in Manchester,' said Ida. 'And you can't do sums! Remember that bother we got into with the grocer when you didn't keep the accounts properly? Why do you want to work in a bank?'

Fa shook his head. 'The truth is that I don't want to work in a bank. I would be hopeless at working in a bank. The bank manager saw that for himself, so no job was offered.'

'Well, I'm glad . . . !' began Ida, but Fa put a hand on her arm.

'No, Ida. I do need to find some kind of employment. We no longer have Mama's allowance from her family, you know.'

Ida jumped up from the sofa.

'Be a fisherman, Fa!' she said. 'We will go back to Norfolk. You'd like fishing, I'm sure, with your own boat and everything! We could eat fish most days, so we wouldn't need much money in any case. I could go back to school, and . . .'

Bong!

The brass gong in the hall was slung between baby elephant tusks. It had been brought from India by Uncle Stephen, and now it had been rung for dinner.

Fa stood up and took a deep breath. 'Well,' he said, 'we are about to find out what your Grandmama's thoughts on the matter are. And I don't think they will involve fishing boats.' Fa held out a hand and grinned at Ida. 'Best of luck, old bean! We'd better face it.'

'Best of luck to you too, old chap!' said Ida as she shook his big hand in hers. 'But remember, Fa, we don't have to do what Grandmama says.'

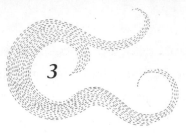

3

Ida had never seen the dining room beyond a peep through an open doorway before. In front of her was a long dark polished table sparkling with silver and cut glass, fruit, and some lilies. There was black ribbon around the vases because the household was in mourning. The lilies were beautiful, thought Ida. Elegant, like Mama. She felt a sudden fondness for the Berringer family for keeping reminders of what had happened to Mama all around the house. That felt right.

The dining room walls were papered in moss-green. Dark heavy, plum-coloured curtains with tassels hung half-drawn across tall windows through which the sun shone. Sliced shafts of sunlight lit up some of the shelves, cabinets and small tables displaying Grandmama's ornaments – china figures, feathery ferns in pots and stuffed birds. The pictures on the walls were pale depictions of Bible scenes, not at all like the colourful landscapes that Fa painted. There were mounted stuffed heads of antelope and tiger, on the wall over the fireplace. Uncle Stephen had shot those poor creatures in India and brought back their heads to England as a present for his mother.

Amid it all was Grandmama at the head of the table.

Grandmama was, of course, dressed in black. She had worn nothing but black since the death of her husband twelve years ago. Since the death of her daughter Isabella, Grandmama's white lacy widow's cap had been replaced with what looked like a black crepe napkin on top of her head. Her hair was a silvery white and her skin properly pale, so the only real colour on Grandmama was her eyes, which were fierce turquoise blue.

Aunts Dora and Helen bustled into the dining room and stood behind chairs on either side of Grandmama. Both aunts looked towards Ida and Fa with the slightly smug air of those who know something that others don't.

Ida bobbed a curtsey. 'Good evening, Grandmama,' she said, her voice sounding strange in the large room. 'I hope that you are well.'

Grandmama inclined her head in a slight nod of acknowledgement. 'Thank you for enquiring, my dear. I am tolerably well, but not as well as I look, you know. My bunions have been quite painful.'

'I'm sorry to hear that, Grandmama.'

That was always the first exchange between Ida and her grandmother. The question and its answer never differed very much.

'Lady Berringer,' said Fa, bending at the waist. 'It is very good of you to include us in your dinner party tonight.'

'It is,' agreed Grandmama. 'I have my reasons, which I shall reveal once we have eaten. Do sit down, everyone.'

Ida sat and looked in awe at the array of cutlery and drinking glasses laid in front of her. As the meal progressed, she was grateful that Aunt Helen felt it her duty to nudge and whisper to make Ida use the correct implement for each eating task she faced.

The food arrived over Ida's left shoulder. The 'simple menu', as Grandmama called it, consisted of cucumber soup, baked turbot, roast wild duck with vegetables and delicious creamy gooseberry fool, followed by cheeses and fruit. Ida tried to do Mama proud by eating daintily and only speaking when spoken to. The grown-ups talked about weather and politics, leaving Ida free to concentrate on the food, but as the last plate was cleared a sudden chill silence made Ida look up. The aunts and Grandmama were all looking at Fa.

'Well?' said Grandmama.

'Oh, well, er . . .' said Fa. 'Um, no. I did not take the job at the bank.'

'Did not take, or were not offered?' asked Aunt Dora, in a sly voice.

Charlotte and Elena have sneaked, thought Ida.

'The post was not offered,' admitted Fa, going red at the collar. 'But the truth is that I would not have suited it, and it would not have suited me. I must think of some other way to earn a living.'

'Indeed you must!' said Grandmama, popping a grape into her mouth and chewing it forcefully.

Ida saw Fa's fists clench. 'I fully intend to make my own way in the world.'

'Exactly how?' Grandmama's icy question hung in the air, unanswered, leaving Fa looking foolish and embarrassed. Grandmama daintily wiped her mouth with her crisp white napkin, then announced, 'No matter. I have corresponded with Stephen and we have it planned.'

Ida saw hurt in Fa's eyes. She opened her mouth to say something, but Aunt Helen's hand, firm on her arm, stopped her as Grandmama continued, 'With Isabella's death has come change for us all. I have asked Dora to put in hand some building works at the Dower House . . .'

Aha, thought Ida! So she *is* going to be nice, for all that she likes to frighten people!

'Thank you, Grandmama,' began Ida. 'That is so very kind of you, but . . .'

'Shush, child!' hissed Aunt Helen.

'. . . because,' said Grandmama, raising a finger to emphasise her point, 'I intend to move into the Dower House directly Stephen is able to free himself from the army and take over here. The Dower House was always intended for the dowager to live in, after all. It is high time that Stephen took over headship of this family, and that entails living in the family seat.'

'But,' said Ida, 'there isn't a spare bedroom in the Dower House, Grandmama. Where would you sleep?'

Grandmama laughed. 'Oh dear me, I am not to move in

with you, Ida my dear. No, no. I shall be living there *instead* of you, with your Aunt Theodora as my companion.'

'That suits us very well, thank you, Grandmama,' smiled Ida. 'Because Fa and I are to go back to Norfolk. You may have the Dower House if you wish.'

Grandmama chuckled. 'You are forgetting, Ida, that the Dower House *is* mine. But you, my dear Ida, are not going back to Norfolk. No. You are to live here in Yewdale Hall, along with your cousins.' Ida felt Aunt Helen stiffen beside her, and realised that maybe this was news to her as well. But Grandmama was still talking.

'Ida is to be sent to a well regarded boarding school in term time. Stephen's girls, of course, have their governess, and Eric will continue at Eton. But Ida will become part of Stephen's family during the holidays. It is what Isabella would have wanted.'

Aunt Helen had gone pale. 'You shall become one of us, Ida,' she said.

Ida looked at Fa who was silent now. 'Is Fa to live in the big house too?'

There was a pause for a moment, then Grandmama said firmly, 'No. What you call the big house will be my son's home, with you as an honorary member of his family, Ida. Your father will be starting a new life elsewhere.'

Fa's voice was quiet, but fierce, as he rose to his feet. 'Madam, I have lost my wife and I have no intention of also losing my daughter. You cannot simply take her as your own.' Tall Fa leaned, challengingly, towards his mother-in-law.

Grandmama didn't flinch. She raised her closed fan and jabbed it towards Fa. 'Do shush, Frank. I shall explain. Sit down.' Fa sat. Grandmama placed her fan beside her plate.

'My family has thought this through most thoroughly.' So 'my family' doesn't include Fa and me, noted Ida bitterly. Maybe it hadn't even included Aunt Helen who, after all, was only a Berringer by marriage. Grandmama sniffed. 'I have decided to settle a sum of money upon you, Frank. A substantial sum, I might add. A generous sum. Offered because my daughter would have wanted me to be generous to you. You are to use the money to start a new life in a new place. You might like to take a living in the church. You could settle in a nice little parish. That would be quite suitable and of course follow in your own father and grandfather's footsteps, if I am not mistaken. You may even find yourself a new wife and raise a new family.'

'How can you even suggest . . . !' Fa was almost spluttering with rage.

Grandmama raised her finger. 'If you are not intending a new family, you should maybe go abroad.'

'Abroad?' said Fa.

'Abroad!' said Ida.

'Abroad,' said Grandmama. 'I suggest South Africa as a suitable destination for a relatively young man with money to invest and no property of his own to keep him at home.'

'South Africa!' Ida stood up now, crashing her chair into the table so that it set the wine and water quivering in their glasses.

'The child has no manners at all!' whispered Aunt Helen.

'Good Lord!' Fa had turned pink. 'Are you trying to pay me off, Lady Berringer? As if, as if, I was some . . . some . . .'

'I am offering you an opportunity and you'd be a fool to turn it down. I am giving your daughter the chance to better herself,and you an opportunity to make something of yourself. Are you going to turn me down?'

'Er, I . . .'

'Fa!' said Ida. 'Don't say "yes". I'd much rather be with you in Norfolk!' But Fa seemed too stunned to speak.

Grandmama cleared her throat. 'So, I will pay for Ida's schooling. And I have here . . .' Grandmama drew something out of the black depths of her dress, '. . . a signed promissory note for a full one thousand guineas, made out to Frank Metcalf, Esquire. Will you take it?'

'No!' said Ida. 'He will not! Fa? Don't!'

Fa took a deep breath.

'Fa!'

'Mind, there are conditions that go with the money.' Grandmama withdrew the note a little. Ida threw down her napkin, knocking over a flower vase, spilling water and lilies over the table.

'Really!' tutted Aunt Dora.

'We shall have to tame her!' said Aunt Helen.

But Ida was already running down the hall, heading for the front door.

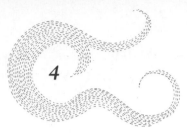

4

Ida heard Fa's steps up the creaky Dower House stairs late that evening.

'Ida?' he called out. 'Are you still up? Can we discuss things, my love?'

Fa pushed open the door of Ida's bedroom. Ida was standing on a chair, reaching up to take a picture from the wall.

'What are you doing?' asked Fa.

'Packing,' said Ida. The picture was one that Fa had done, a picture of gorse and pebbles and sand seen from their Norfolk home. She put the picture on top of the tumble of clothes that she had already thrown into an open trunk.

'But they'll send people from the big house to move your belongings up there, I'm sure. There's no need to do this.' Fa held out his arms. 'Come down to the kitchen for a mug of cocoa. I want to talk to you.'

'I am not going to live with them up there, whatever Grandmama thinks. I am going back to Norfolk. With you, Fa.'

Fa fiddled with the pebbles that Ida had arranged along her windowsill.

'We can't do that.'

'Yes, we can! You took Grandmama's money, didn't you? So we can afford to buy a house of our own.' Ida stopped packing. 'Let's go tonight! Please, Fa? Eloping, just as you and Mama did. That worked out, didn't it?'

Fa smiled, but shook his head. 'Grandmama's money comes with conditions. Since I won't go into the church, I must go abroad.' Fa's big hand stroked Ida's hair. 'It won't be for long. Not more than a year or two. I shall probably go to Africa . . .'

'Then I shall come with you!' Ida shook Fa's sleeve. 'I would love to visit Africa!'

'This isn't a holiday trip, or one suitable for children,' said Fa. 'I will be amongst rough, primitive kinds of people, and there will be diseases and nobody of your own kind. There is even a threat of fresh fighting out there.'

'But I don't . . . !' began Ida, but Fa put a finger to her lips.

'Your mama wanted you to be brought up as a young lady, and that is what Grandmama and Uncle Stephen and Aunt Helen are offering. It might not be what you or I want, but it is, nevertheless, a generous offer. I want you to accept it, for Mama's sake.' Ida was silenced.

Fa took her hands into his own big ones. 'Walking home just now I was thinking and, you know, it really is quite exciting.' He squeezed Ida's hands and she saw a spark in his eyes. She knew that Mama would love the fact that

Fa was properly excited about something for the first time in months. 'I could become a farmer in Kenya, growing maize, or raising cattle or somesuch. I really must find out exactly what.'

'But you don't know anything at all about farming,' said Ida.

'Then maybe I would do better in the diamond mining business in South Africa?' Fa held up Ida's hand, kissed it and laughed. 'Oh, I shall bring you back diamonds, my Ida, and have them made into so many rings that all the ladies at the big house will be green with envy! How about that, eh?'

Ida didn't have the heart not to smile back.

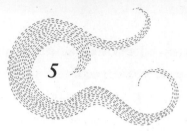

5

But Fa wasn't talking about diamond mining next morning.

'Look at this!' he said, waving the newspaper. '"Trustworthy reports state that the district is extremely rich in gold." How about that?'

'What district?'

'The Yukon valley, in Canada. Gold was apparently found in large quantities last year, but the place freezes solid over their long winter, so the miners with their gold, and news of their find didn't get out until this spring. Now the ports are full of the scruffiest looking men you could possibly imagine, but rich as anything, all of them lugging tatty great suitcases and sacks and jars full of golden nuggets and gold dust. Imagine! It's reported that people are travelling to Alaska from Britain now, looking to make their fortunes. It seems there's still plenty of gold to be found.'

'Gosh!' said Ida. 'Just like California in one of Eric's books. That had a gold rush.'

'That's exactly it,' said Fa. 'But this time it's around the Klondike River.' Fa jabbed a finger at the newspaper. 'Ha! There's a bit about Canadians and Americans fighting over who owns the land where the gold is. It is in Canada, but most prospectors are going through American Alaska to get there.' Fa grinned. 'Think of it, Ida: the Klondike actually lies in part of our British Empire. It's ours! Fetch down the atlas, and let's see if we can find the place.'

'Why isn't everybody in the world rushing there, if there really is so much gold to take?' asked Ida, as she pulled the big book off the shelf.

'Ah!' Fa flipped through its pages, stopping when he came to a map of North America. 'That is because the Klondike isn't at all an easy place to get to.' He ran a finger northwards up the western coast of America, up to an area with just a very few place names on the coast, and none at all inland.

'Even those already in America or Canada have a very hazardous journey if they want to get that far north. It's almost in the Arctic. No roads, no shops, and temperatures low enough to freeze mercury, so I read.' Fa ran a finger along a line in the newspaper. '"Provisions are scarce and dear, if procurable at all." In fact, they advise people not to go. "... all persons are strongly warned against attempting it."' Fa folded the paper shut. 'I imagine that it must cost a great deal of money just to get there, so you would need a fair bit of wealth before you could even have the chance to look for gold. Ah, well.'

Ida sat up. 'But, Fa, you have got wealth! You've got Grandmama's money!'

'Well, that's true enough,' said Fa. He got up from his

chair. It was the maid's day off. 'Shall I make us cheese on toast for lunch?' offered Fa. 'Tilly brought some raspberries from the big house, so we can have those for a pudding.'

Ida nodded. She'd taken the newspaper and spread it out on the rug in front of the empty fireplace. That 'Klondike' word jumped out at her from amongst the advertisements.

'Fa, what is a syndicate?' asked Ida.

Fa was clattering with pans and plates in the scullery. 'It's a sort of club, I suppose. A group of people getting together to pool their money into one really big sum. Are you hungry? Do you want one slice or two?'

'Just one, please. But what does the club do with that money?'

'They use it for some enterprise, and any riches resulting will be shared between the members of the syndicate, according to the amount of money they put in. Why do you ask?'

'Because it says in the newspaper that you can join a syndicate for finding gold. Shares are ten pounds each. So you could buy shares and get gold, but still stay in England with me!'

'Ouch! Damnation!' came Fa's voice from the kitchen. She heard him throw down the knife. Ida jumped up to find Fa clutching his finger.

'I'll make the lunch,' said Ida. She took over cutting the bread and placed the slices on the hot stove.

'Let me see that,' said Fa.

Fa sucked his finger and read while Ida melted grated cheese with an egg and a little mustard in the milk pan. She poured the melted cheese onto the toast and popped it into the oven to brown.

'It says here,' said Fa, '"To Gentlemen with moderate Capital (number limited to sixty) for proposed industrial settlement of income-paying homesteads in South Africa on line of rail to Cape Town and all markets." It promises a "good income".'

'That sounds boring compared to goldfields,' said Ida.

Fa laughed. 'It isn't a matter of gold growing in fields like a crop of corn,' he said. 'I believe that finding and extracting the gold is exceedingly hard work.'

'It is,' said Ida. 'Mama and I read about how they did it in California. The gold is in the soil, a bit like dust. You have to wash and wash the soil – tons of it – to get the gold out of it. You can do it in a rocker, like a giant baby's cradle. Or in little handfuls in a gold pan, but that takes even longer.'

'Really?' Fa looked at Ida with astonishment. 'You and Mama read about that? That does sound exceedingly hard work, especially in a place where the ground is frozen solid for much of the year.'

Suddenly the light from the open garden doorway was blocked. A shadow fell over Fa as Aunt Helen's voice declared, 'And exceedingly hard work is not something that Frank Metcalf has been noted for.'

'Not now, Helen,' scolded Grandmama, pushing past her daughter-in-law.

'Oh! How are you, Grandmama?' asked Ida, bobbing a curtsey. 'I hope that you are well. And . . . and what are you doing here, Grandmama?' Ida knew that was an impertinent question to ask, but the words were out of her mouth before she could stop them.

'I am well, thank you, my dear. Although not as well as I look. My bunions are bad, but I'm bearing up. I have come to ascertain when my home will be ready for Mr Smollet. And I came to see whether my granddaughter has all she needs before setting off for school.'

Fa bent rather stiffly towards his mother-in-law. 'Lady Berringer,' he said. Then he nodded at his sister-in-law. 'And the other Lady Berringer. Good afternoon to you both. Um, Ida and I were about to share a lunch of cheese on toast. I don't suppose that we could tempt you to join us?'

Aunt Helen looked disgusted. 'I should think not! Cook will have a suitable meal awaiting us, thank you all the same.'

But Grandmama lifted her face and sniffed the air like a rabbit. 'Ah, so that explains the aroma, so familiar to me from my childhood. Do you know, Ida, my nanny used to have cheese on toast made for us for nursery tea sometimes. It was my very favourite.' She hesitated, consulted the timepiece that hung from a ribbon on her dress front, and glanced at Aunt Helen. 'I do believe that I that will share a little of your lunch, if you are quite sure that you have spare. Helen you may take the coach home and tell James to come back for me in an hour's time.'

Grandmama sat at the gate-legged table in the kitchen while Ida took the cheese on toast from the oven. She cut the toast into pieces so that she could share them between three plates without it being too obvious that a helping for two was being shared with another.

'Would you like to try some chutney with yours, Grandmama?' asked Ida.

'I would!' said Grandmama. 'And a couple of those very nice looking tomatoes, if you please!'

'Fa grew those in the garden,' said Ida.

'Did he, indeed?' said Grandmama.

So the three of them sat and ate their meal, chatting rather stiffly about nothing of any great importance. When Grandmama had finished, she put her knife and fork neatly side by side on her plate. She dabbed her mouth with the napkin that Ida had, thankfully, found in a drawer.

'Well!' she said. 'I surprise myself by declaring that to have been a most delicious lunch. Thank you, Ida my dear. You are quite the little cook. And, Frank, you clearly have gardening skills. Thank you both.'

'You're very welcome,' said Ida. She was about to jump up and clear the plates, but Grandmama put a hand on her arm.

'Now, what I really want to know is what you two were discussing when I arrived at the door. Something about frozen ground and babies' cradles – most intriguing!'

'Oh,' said Fa, 'it was something in the newspaper about the rush of people heading for the Klondike, looking for gold.'

'Oh, that! The silly greedy fools,' said Grandmama. 'To risk life and limb in such a gamble, you would have to be a very fool, would you not?' Grandmama looked at Fa. Fa lifted his chin. Oh dear, thought Ida.

'Frank!' said Grandmama. 'You are surely not thinking of joining them? I don't approve of gambling, you know.'

'I don't see that hunting for gold is any more of a gamble than hunting for diamonds,' said Fa.

'It is utterly different!' declared Grandmama, hands neatly folded on her lap. 'Gentlemen owning diamond mines do not dig the ground for diamonds themselves. They employ natives to do the labouring.'

'Surely it is more honourable to work for yourself rather than using others to do your work for you?' said Fa. 'In fact, I think that there should be British men prepared to bring that gold home. It seems to me to be a noble venture.'

'Noble!' said Grandmama. 'I think you'd find that it is common low-life kinds of people who are drawn to that place.'

Fa's neck had gone red. 'But then, you do regard me

as being rather "common" and "low", do you not, Lady Berringer?' Fa's eyes flashed.

Oh, don't say that, Fa! thought Ida. Not when Grandmama has been nice over the lunch! But Fa couldn't stop. His arms were waving.

'The Klondike must surely be just the place for me!'

'I very much doubt you could manage in such a place!' said Grandmama with a sniff.

Ida glared at Grandmama. 'Fa will go there if he says that he will!'

Grandmama's eyebrows made little arches of surprise. 'Well, I shall watch with interest.' She rose from the chair. 'My carriage is waiting. Goodbye, Ida my dear. I look forward to our getting better acquainted once you are resident at Yewdale Hall.' Grandmama put a finger under Ida's chin. 'You interest me.'

Fa and Ida rose from their chairs. Grandmama raised a hand in farewell. 'I shall send Tilly to help pack your things.'

'Oh,' said Ida. 'How soon must . . . ?'

'Tomorrow would suit very well,' said Grandmama.

'Tomorrow!' said Ida. 'But I want to stay with Fa until he has to go.'

'I will allow that.' Grandmama took the stick that Ida held out for her. 'But your departure, to wherever you settle upon, must not be delayed, Frank.' She gave him a firm look. 'A fortnight at most!'

6

That evening, Ida found the book about the Californian gold rush that she and Mama had read together: Captain Bayley's Heir by G.A. Henty. She flipped the pages until she found a picture of men working a 'rocker' to extract gold from 'dirt'. Ida noticed that the men working the rocker had guns slung from their belts. Ida's heart thumped in her chest. Would Fa be amongst men with guns?

Ida read the book's text, finding a description of 'the saloons where gambling went on from morning 'til night, broken only by the occasional fierce quarrel, followed in most cases by the sharp crack of a revolver, or by desperate encounters with bowie knives'. It seemed that Grandmama was right about the kinds of people who went prospecting! And Fa was a man who could lose his temper so easily, he was bound to get into a quarrel. If there were guns and knives and drink involved, terrible things might happen!

Oh, she should have stopped him from saying what he did to Grandmama. Mama would have! But instead, she, Ida, had encouraged Fa to say that he would go prospecting, so his going to the Klondike was her fault. But there was no getting out of it now – not without Grandmama and the aunts sneering.

'I shall just have to go with him,' decided Ida.

'Absolutely not!' said Fa, when she told him. 'It'll be far too dangerous for a child. We have already been through this, Ida. You are to go to boarding school and live in the big house.'

'But . . .'

'And that is an end to it!'

No, it's not, thought Ida.

In what felt like a frightening, exciting rush of days, Fa prepared for his trip. He went to Manchester to buy supplies and tickets and he came home full of stories.

'There are fellows coming out of the Klondike district with between thirty and seventy thousand dollars' worth of gold each. Think of it!' said Fa, arms waving like shirtsleeves on a windy washing line. 'Not everyone comes away with so much gold, of course, especially now that the easy pickings have gone. But the dominion surveyor himself is reporting that miners are taking gold to a value of well over a thousand pounds each day that they work. Imagine that! It won't take me too long to bag a worthwhile hoard. Then I will come home to my Ida and we can buy ourselves that house in Norfolk that you so long for.'

Fa bought leather hiking boots and a tweed jacket and thick socks, gloves and long underwear.

'They tell me that I shall have to buy what they call an "outfit" once I reach Canada,' Fa told Ida, his eyes bright with excitement. 'Food and equipment, tents and shovels and such. But there's little point in lugging too much over the Atlantic and the continent when I can buy what's needed nearer my destination.'

Fa paid a man a large sum of money for a steamship ticket.

'He's done marvellously well for me,' said Fa. 'Got me the last ticket of all on a Norwegian ship going from Liverpool to Quebec.'

'When do you sail?' asked Ida.

'Travelling to Liverpool on the twelfth, then steaming away westwards on the thirteenth. The ship is due in Quebec on twenty-third August, so that gives time to get across the continent, and maybe to the Klondike itself, before winter sets in. I shall be all set up and ready to begin prospecting once the spring thaw comes. I'm told that most other chaps are planning on setting off next spring so I shall be ahead of their game, even if I am behind those who are already Klondike-bound.'

'It says in the newspaper,' Ida read out loud, 'that there will be thirty thousand miners on the headwaters of the Klondike before winter. Thirty thousand, Fa!'

'Then I shall have to go faster than any of the rest of them,' said Fa, with a big grin. 'It's a race for treasure after all.'

Ida's mind whirled. How, how, how, was she going to get onto that boat, along with Fa, in order to keep him safe and her out of boarding school?

Ida counted the savings that she kept in a purse hidden at the back of a drawer. Six shillings, sixpence and a farthing.

'How much does your boat ticket cost, Fa?'

'I can't remember exactly, but something in the order of a hundred pounds. That's for a return ticket, of course. And first class.'

A hundred pounds! That was an impossible sum for Ida to find. Even travelling steerage with the poorer classes would apparently cost as much as ten pounds for just one way. Ida supposed that she could rely on Fa to pay for her return fare. But she didn't even have a single whole pound. With a horrible lurch of her stomach, Ida suddenly realised something exciting and frightening – she would have to stow away.

Ida had read about stowaways hiding under upturned lifeboats until the ship was too far out at sea to make it worth its while turning back.

'Fa?'

'Yes.'

'Can I go with you to Liverpool so that I can wave you off?'

'And how would you get back here, all on your own, once I had sailed? I don't think that's a good idea.

But as Fa looked at maps and timetables and lists of equipment and made lots of notes, so too did Ida.

'Where exactly is my new school?' she asked.

'St Margaret's? It's in Shrewsbury,' said Fa. 'They do say that it's a very good school.'

'But Liverpool is on the way to Shrewsbury, and you go the same date that I am supposed to arrive at St Margaret's, so I could easily see you off.'

Fa opened his long arms and hugged her. 'Well, if that is what you really want, it will certainly be nice for me.'

Fa and Mr Baines from the big house, packed most of his and Ida's belongings into tea chests, ready to go into storage. Fa sang as he packed a large leather suitcase for his Klondike expedition. Ida packed too. Aunt Helen had sent down a brand new trunk and Ida packed for school – plain dresses and lots of petticoats and underdrawers and handkerchiefs, sheets and towels and books of grammar and natural history, a shawl and new buttoned boots. She let Aunt Helen inspect and approve her packing because it didn't matter.

The packing might be going to St Margaret's, but Ida was not.

7

Grandmama summoned Ida up to the main house for a farewell tea on the lawn. Grandmama wore a big hat to keep off the sun.

'How are you, Grandmama? I hope that you are well,' said Ida, bobbing a curtsey.

'Not as well as I look, my dear,' said Grandmama, holding out a hand to take Ida's in her own. 'But my bunions need not concern you. Goodness you do have a look of Isabella about you today.' She gave Ida's hand a little shake. 'You are to apply yourself to learning all that they have to teach in school. Tame that temper you've inherited from your father, and I'm sure that you will do very well.'

'Thank you, Grandmama.' Ida sat in the cane chair.

'I have something for you,' said Grandmama, pointing to a small package on Ida's side of the table. 'A small gift.'

Ida hesitated.

'You may open it,' said Grandmama. So Ida slid the ribbon from the long thin box and lifted the lid to reveal a fine fountain pen.

'It is made of mother of pearl,' said Grandmama. 'I thought it pretty. I would like you to write me a weekly letter, telling how you are progressing at St Margaret's.' Grandmama gave a small nod and a smile. 'I shall look forward to reading your news. I never went to school and my daughters had a governess, so it will all be novel to me. A little adventure!'

'Of course, Grandmama,' said Ida. But I won't be at St Margaret's, she thought. I will be stowed away on a boat. What will you think of me then, Grandmama?

'You know, Grandmama, I really could travel to St Margaret's on my own. It is very kind of you to lend Tilly, but there is no need.'

Grandmama laughed. 'I know that you have been brought up to some strange ways, but no granddaughter of mine is going to travel alone on the public trains. Now, do pass those cucumber sandwiches before they curl in the heat.'

Oh dear, thought Ida. However am I going to escape from Tilly and get onto that boat?

Ida's trunk of school things had been strapped and labelled and sent to St Margaret's School ahead of her. So, that evening, Ida packed a few things that she had managed to keep out of the trunk. Tilly had told her to pack a carpet bag for their overnight stay in Liverpool, so now Ida added some winter stockings and a woollen liberty bodice to the nightgown and flannel and toothbrush. She added Duffle too, the worn old toy dog that Mama had made for her so long ago. Then she stuffed in a coat that had been handed down to her by Aunt Helen.

'Charlotte declares that she will no longer wear it since blue does not suit her. I thought that it might be of use to you, Ida, once the weather becomes colder.'

It was a good woollen winter coat, dark blue and with an extra cape over the shoulders in the fashion worn by highwaymen in illustrated stories. On that hot August evening Ida found it hard to think of cold weather. But the coat could be a blanket for the nights on the boat. I'll need food as well, and certainly something to drink. She found a bottle of ginger beer in the kitchen and took the last hunk of a fruitcake and some cheese from the larder. She wrapped both in a clean tea towel and rammed them into the bag too.

'Come and talk to me, Ida,' called Fa from the empty parlour. The room was eerily echoey with its furnishings gone, but strangely beautiful in the candlelight. Fa was standing by the window, looking out towards the moonlit church. He turned as Ida came in.

'This is our last evening in a home we have shared with Mama.' Ida wrapped her arms around Fa and rested her head against his back.

'It is an end, but also a beginning,' he said.

'Mmm,' said Ida.

8

A hansom cab carried Fa and Tilly and Ida and their luggage away from the Berringer estate and the village and the church, through fields and villages to Manchester. There the swaying, jolting cab came to a stop. They climbed out and entered the grand station building, full of crowds and noise. Ida kept tight hold of her bag as a porter helped them to the right platform and into carriages behind the great hissing steaming engine.

'Fa,' said Ida. 'What exactly happens tomorrow? What time do you get onto that boat?'

'Well, the first thing I have to do is to meet my man with the boat ticket. I can't hope to get very far without that!'

'No.' But that is exactly what I intend to do, thought Ida, and she felt a little sick.

A whistle blew and, with a lurch, they were off – steaming and puffing out of Manchester, heading towards Liverpool and the sea.

They stayed the night in the modern Railway Hotel in Liverpool. Horse-drawn trams ran alongside the hotel, rumbling their wheels along metal grooves. Ida lay awake in the big hotel bed, listening to the strange city nighttime noises, and puzzling as to how she was going to get aboard

Fa's boat. She still hadn't worked out how it was to be done as the sky began to lighten behind the heavy hotel curtains.

Fa and Ida breakfasted in the big dining room, waited on by men in stiff white coats offering great silver platters of kedgeree and kidneys, bread and butter, honey and marmalade. It was a treat, but Ida couldn't feel hungry. You must eat all you can while you have the chance, she told herself, but she somehow couldn't. Fa looked at her.

'I am sad too,' he said. 'But this is an adventure for me, and another kind of adventure for you.'

Ida nodded. 'Fa, when is that man coming with your ticket?'

'He said he would meet me here at nine thirty.' Fa pulled his watch from his waistcoat pocket. 'He's running late, but never mind, eh? More time for us to enjoy breakfast together!'

Time ticked on, but the man didn't appear; Ida began to see how things could work out nicely now. They could sneak off to Norfolk and Grandmama need never know!

Fa went to the hotel reception desk to ask if anybody had been enquiring for a Mr Metcalf. They hadn't.

'No sign at all of that wretched man,' Fa told Ida. 'And time and tide won't wait . . .'

'I'll fetch my bag so as to be ready when he does arrive,' said Ida. Tilly was tidying things in Ida's room. Ida picked up her bag.

'Oh, there's no need for you to carry that, Miss,' began Tilly, but Ida held on to it.

'I, er, I want to give something to Fa before he goes. Could you wait here just a minute or two, please, Tilly?'

'Want a moment alone with your father before you part?' smiled Tilly. 'Of course, Miss.'

'Thank you very much,' said Ida, and she hurried back to the hotel lift.

But Ida knew that it wouldn't be long before Tilly followed her down. And she knew that Tilly would chase her all the way to Norfolk and drag her back to Grandmama.

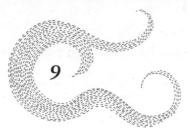

9

Fa was flapping around the hotel lobby like a trapped bird.

'Oh, Ida, there you are. I don't think the wretched man is coming at all. He has conned me out of the hundred guineas he took for my ticket. Oh, I am such a gullible fool! Your Grandmama has the proper measure of me, Ida. I am a veritable fool!'

Suddenly, Ida knew just what to do. She took Fa by the arm. 'You still have a great deal of money from Grandmama, so you can buy another ticket for the boat.'

'But it was the last . . .'

'That man didn't tell you the truth. You know that now!'

'Well, maybe . . .' Fa lifted his pocket watch and looked at it. 'I suppose there might still be time . . .'

'There is time!' said Ida. 'And I am going too, to find gold with you.'

'Don't be ridiculous, Ida! I've already said . . .'

'If you don't take me with you now, then I will go back and tell Grandmama and the aunts and everybody else that Frank Metcalf failed in his quest before he even left this country!'

'You surely wouldn't . . .'

'I would, Fa, I really would!' Ida was laughing now. 'This is perfect!'

'It is all very far from perfect,' muttered Fa, but he let Ida steer him towards the door.

'Ask the concierge to stop a cab for us.'

'What about . . .' Fa was dithering, hands fluttering like an injured bird's wings by his sides. 'I'm really not sure this is . . .'

'Go!'

There was hotel writing paper and a pencil on the reception desk, so Ida wrote:

> *Dear Tilly,*
>
> *Please do not be cross. The fact is, I am to go with Fa to Canada. It is my idea, not his. Please tell Grandmama that Fa has done nothing wrong, but don't tell even that until after our boat has left port. You know that school and I would not have got on. Mama always said that one should live every moment of life, so I am. I shall tell you about the Klondike and the gold some day, when we are home again.*
>
> *Very fondest regards,*
> *Ida Metcalf*

She left the note with the man on the desk. Tilly was bound to come looking for them soon.

Then, like thieves on the run, Ida and Fa hurried to get into a Hackney cab.

'To the docks!' Fa instructed the driver. 'The ticket office for the Allan Line. Quick as you like!'

Ida grasped Fa's arm. He looked at her and grinned. 'Oh, Ida, I think that this might be fun!'

10

Fa got tickets for the steamer SS *Austrian*, sailing on the next tide, en route from Norway to Quebec in Canada.

'Last minute cancellations,' said Fa. 'Tickets for second-class cabins. We must board at once.'

'Which ship?' asked Ida, because the huge docks seemed full of ships of different kinds.

'I was told to look for a red, black and white funnel. Ah, that must be her!' Fa pointed.

'Really?'

The ship was enormous. It had three layers of portholes along its hull, with white cabins on top, all slung with lifeboats. There was a mast either end of the ship, but the huge red funnel dominated the centre, smoke already rising dirtily out of it. The whole ship throbbed with engine power.

Ida and Fa followed the boy carrying their bags up the gangplank, and Ida realised that a great weight had lifted from her. I have a ticket! There's no need to stow away after all. Oh, I must make sure to enjoy this, she thought.

A steward showed them to their cabins. Single gentlemen and unmarried girls were on separate floors, so Ida found herself in a cabin with two smiley ladies who spoke only Norwegian. It was a neat little room with narrow beds hanging off the walls, lots of polished wood and brasswork, and a porthole through which she could see the grey-brown water slopping about. Have any drops of that sea visited Norfolk, wondered Ida?

Fa and Ida stood on deck with all the other passengers, watching and waving, cheering, or weeping quietly, as the ship slipped away from the dock and Liverpool shrank into the distance. Ida waved goodbye to . . . she wasn't sure who or what. England. Her old life. Mama. The life that Grandmama and the aunts had planned for her.

'Well, my Ida, whatever have we gone and done?' asked Fa with a grin.

'Escaped,' said Ida.

'That is rather how it feels,' said Fa. 'What lies ahead, I wonder? Neither you nor I know much about living in Arctic conditions. Nor the mining of gold.'

'I know something about mining,' said Ida. 'I have got Eric's book in my bag. You can read it, if you like.'

'The Klondike is very different from California,' said Fa. 'And, oh Lord, you haven't any suitable clothes with you. We will have to buy it all in Canada.' His forehead furrowed. 'And there are two of us to pay for now.'

'Sorry, Fa.' Ida felt her first twinge of guilt. 'I won't need so very much to eat.'

'Ha!' Fa wrapped long arms around Ida and held her close. 'You will need a great deal to eat if you are to keep out the cold. But you will cheer and help me, I am sure.'

The ship called in at an Irish port to pick up the last of its passengers and cargo, then they were off into the seemingly endless sea that lay between Ireland and America.

They saw the odd dolphin leaping beside the ship and birds flying overhead, but otherwise it was sea, sea, sea.

Fa played chess with some of the men. 'It really doesn't matter that we don't understand a thing the other says,' Fa told Ida. 'We all speak chess.'

Ida tried talking with the women in her cabin. She learnt that *nynorsk* meant 'hello' and *takk* meant 'thank you' in Norwegian. She taught the women a few English words, but mostly they all just pointed and smiled, or did a little mime, if they had something that they wanted to communicate. She read Eric's Captain Bayley book, then swapped it with another English girl for a book about life in a boarding school, which made her wonder if the adventures to be had at school mightn't be more exciting than those to be found in a search for gold.

Fa and Ida could dine together, although neither of them was properly hungry once they were on the open sea and the boat was heaving through buffeting waves. It seemed that everyone went down with seasickness sooner or later. Putting on her blue coat and pacing the deck helped.

Fa and Ida went to the prayer meetings. Ida thought of Mama and prayed for Mama's soul in Heaven. She prayed for what lay ahead for Fa and herself. She thought about Tilly and Grandmama.

'Can letters be sent from the ship?' asked Ida.

'Not until we get into port, when they can be left at a post office. Who do you want to write to?'

'Grandmama,' said Ida.

'Really?'

'I promised her,' said Ida.

'Then you must do it,' agreed Fa.

So Ida tore paper from the exercise book she had in her bag. She took out her pen, and wrote:

21 August 1897

Dear Grandmama,

I hope that this finds you well.

Please do not be disappointed that I have not after all gone to school. I feel sure that I can learn more by travelling the world and trying new ventures. And I do want to help Fa.

Let me tell you about life on board ship. We drink coffee boiled with treacle and it is delicious. It helps cure seasickness, which has been a problem since we got out onto open sea. Perhaps Cook could make some for you when you are feeling less well than you look? We are given plum pudding on Sundays, which puts me in mind of Christmas, even though it is still summer. We have been at sea for so long now that the ship's daily routine feels extraordinarily ordinary.

Because this is a Norwegian ship, most of the people on board are Norwegian. There are also lots of Irish people, as well as some English who boarded with us in Liverpool. Most of the people are going to start new lives in Canada. Some, I think, are going to look for gold as we are. Those looking for gold are called argonauts. Doesn't that sound grand!

We are in the second week at sea and getting near to Newfoundland. We have seen ice floating and it has become cold. Please thank Aunt Helen and Charlotte for my good coat. We have had some rough seas, when the wind moans and the water crashes. Some passengers are scared by the storms, but I find that I like them. They make water jump out of my glass tumbler at dinner. I have seen seals swimming. Fa says that this steamship goes twice as fast as a sailing ship. That is important because we must get to the gold before it is all gone.

Thank you for this pen. I will keep my promise to write to you again.

Your granddaughter,
Ida Metcalf

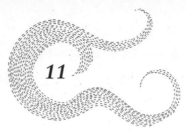

11

After ten days at sea – 'See that?' Fa pointed. The horizon seemed to have been painted with a thicker brush than it had a short time before. 'Land!'

They steamed past islands and coastline and into the narrower and narrower mouth of the St Lawrence River. The ship slowed and people leaned on the sides to watch as they gently approached, and finally touched with a bump, the solid land of Canada.

It was 23 August, a chill blustery day that felt full of fresh possibilities. There was paperwork to be gone through, and Fa's luggage to be reclaimed, but Ida was almost wriggling with impatience to get off the ship.

'Come on, Fa! It's a race, remember!'

'Yes, yes,' said Fa, picking up his heavy leather suitcase. 'But I don't speak French well and . . .'

'Come on!' said Ida.

When they got to the ticket office at the railway station they pointed at posters and timetables, pointed at themselves and their bags. They said *s'il vous plais* and *merci* and smiled a lot. The man behind the counter listened and nodded. He let them carry on for some time before grinning broadly and saying,

'Visiting the West Coast, are you, sir?'

'Gracious!' laughed Fa. 'You're as English as I am!'

'From London, Sir. East End. Came here for a better life.'

'Oh,' said Fa. 'Yes, we are heading to the Klondike, also looking to make a better life for ourselves. Two tickets, please.'

The man's eyebrows shot up his forehead. 'Really, sir? I'm not sure the Klondike is the kind of place it would be advisable to take a young lady, if you don't mind me saying. I've seen prospectors, and they are all sorts and ranks of person, but never yet a fine young lady.'

'Oh dear,' said Fa.

'The train to the west coast won't be so bad, except for the quality of company on it,' said the clerk. 'But I would recommend taking the boat up the coast. That way there'll be no call for the young lady to climb mountains.'

'Indeed,' said Fa, pulling out his wallet.

'There's an extra 'gold rush' car being attached to the next train from Montreal to Vancouver,' said the clerk. 'But you might do better to go first class with the young lady.'

Fa clasped his wallet and dithered. He's thinking of the cost, thought Ida, so she told the man, 'The gold rush car will suit us very well. We must save our money for buying clothing and food, and for the boat trip.'

The man laughed. 'I wish my wife had your attitude, Miss! I can see you're of a practical nature!'

Fa raised his hands in a gesture of resignation. 'Indeed! Gold rush men are the people we will be living amongst soon enough. We will take tickets for your gold rush car, please.'

Fa and Ida shoved their luggage into overhead racks and settled into their seats. The carriage was crowded with men talking loudly in French and English and Chinese, but they went suddenly quiet when they noticed Ida. Ida sat back on the hard wooden seat. She could feel them all staring at her. Fa cleared his throat.

'Gentlemen,' he said. 'May I introduce my daughter, Miss Ida Metcalf. She is travelling to the Klondike with me. I am sure that you will all treat her kindly and respectfully. Thank you.' There were grunts of acknowledgement from all around. Ida looked at the floor. Please let the train get moving and the men get talking again, she thought. We have got a thousand miles to go across Canada, I want to see it all. Then I will write and tell Grandmama how it is to cross a continent.

As soon as the great engine huff-puffed into noisy motion, clattering over rails going westwards, the talk started up again between the men. They talked of their plans. A dapper little man in a strange tartan suit and twirly moustache intended to dig for gold all next summer then,

'If I've not made my fortune finding gold, I shall teach the miners to dance through the cold and dark of winter.

I don't mind which makes more – the mining or the dancing – but, one way or the other, I intend to return home a richer man!'

A couple of brothers in rough clothes said they were leaving their parents to run the family farm for a year. They hoped to find enough gold to ensure that they'd neither of them ever have to work the farm again. 'Nor the old folks, neither.'

'We're reckoning on plain hard work gaining the most,' they said.

But there was another man who had a different idea about how to make his fortune.

'I have it all worked out,' he told them. 'Common sense tells me that those particles of gold floating down the streams must be comin' from somewhere. There has to be a blame great mountain of gold that the small stuff comes off – the mother lode is what they're calling it, and I'm planning on finding it. I know jist where to look for it too.'

Ida part-closed her eyes and pretended to snooze. The men talked more freely and more interestingly when they thought she wasn't listening. 'Where is this mother lode to be found, then?' asked someone.

'Yes, I'd be most interested to . . .' began Fa. But:

'I ain't telling any one of yous!' laughed the man. 'I ain't giving away my fortune to any one of yous, no siree!'

Then why are you telling about it, wondered Ida? The mother-lode man must either be a fool, putting himself in danger with his boasting or, thought Ida, he's being clever and playing some kind of game.

Ida smelled strong drink as a flask was passed across the carriage and she felt Fa stiffen with disapproval beside her. Peeping through part-closed eyelids she saw the mother-lode man take a swig, then laugh a whisky-scented guffaw.

'My thanks for the drink, but you've underestimated me if you're supposing that drink will loosen my tongue. It'd take twenty barrels of whisky before I told a soul what I know!'

So that's his game, thought Ida, as even the brothers who looked as though they had nothing to spare offered the man sandwiches. 'You'll surely need good strong men to work with you if you're to bring all that gold back home,' they said.

Ida felt Fa's protective arm curl around her, and hug her safe to him, as the talk got louder and the day darkened to night outside the carriage.

Over the days, Ida learned all sorts about the Klondike from talk in the carriage. Apparently the Canadian Mounted Police checked that every man had a ton of goods before he was allowed into Yukon territory. There were taxes to be paid, gangsters to be ware of, different techniques for digging 'pay dirt' with gold in it, and different ways of getting the gold out of that dirt. A quiet man next to Fa told them that he was a doctor from New York, where times were hard just now.

'The rich getting richer while the poor get poorer, and I was a doctor to the poor,' he told them. 'So I'm new to this game, just as you are.' He showed them a book. 'Newly published by the Chicago Record newspaper,' he said. 'They have reporters in the region, so I believe this can be relied upon to be up-to-date and honest in its information.'

Fa read the Chicago Record's 'Book For Gold-Seekers', and made notes.

'Oh, dear,' sighed Fa.

'What is it?'

'We have left it too late to go by steamer up the Yukon River this year,' Fa told her.

'That's right,' said the mother-lode man. 'Freezin' up for the winter jist about now. Won't be a thing movin' up or down that river for months to come.'

'Dash it!' said Fa. 'I really can't have you climbing mountains and carrying goods, Ida. And all in the coldest kind of conditions.' The thought scared Ida too. But it was her fault that she was here, not Fa's.

'I'm strong,' she told him.

The book detailed the different routes into the remote area where gold could be found. It had pictures, taken from photographs, that showed tents in snowy blizzards. And it listed what should be bought for a prospector's outfit: stove, buckets, knife, fork, spoon, cup and plate, frying pan, coffee pot, sharpening stone, two picks and one shovel, whipsaw, pack strap, woollen clothes, boots and shoes, snow glasses, matches, soup, vegetables, butter (canned), bacon, flour, rolled oats, beans, tea and coffee, sugar, dried potatoes, dried onions, salt, pepper, dried fruit, baking powder, evaporated vinegar, soap, hatchet, nails, files, axe, chisels, butcher's knife, hammer, compass, lash rope, pitch, blankets, tent, mosquito netting, canvas . . . and, of course, a gold pan.

Ida couldn't imagine how she and Fa could ever carry all that, but it must be possible because all of the men on the train were intending to do just that, and many others had done it already.

'There are sure to be horses we can hire. Or the book mentions Indians who will porter the stuff for a payment,' said Fa. 'We must thank your Grandmama for providing the money that can pay for such help.' He patted Ida rather clumsily on her head as if she were a pet dog. 'All will be well,' he told her. 'It will.'

But Ida saw the creases on his forehead. If they spent money on horses or porters, would there still be enough money left to pay for their journey home? We absolutely must find gold when we get there, thought Ida. She looked around the carriage and saw on the men's faces that every one of them was thinking that they absolutely must find gold too.

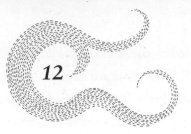

12

It thrilled Ida to think that somewhere back in England, thousands of miles away, was the ghost of the Ida who should have been sitting in some dull classroom – full of bored girls, watching a teacher pointing a cane at a map on the wall. All while the real Ida was travelling the actual world. She gazed and gazed out of the windows.

It was all so interesting. At every railway station they saw Chinese men working as porters.

'Thousands came from China as labourers to build this railway,' Fa told her. 'Some of them have stayed and made their homes here. And some headed for the gold fields, just like us.'

'They will be better at digging for gold than we are,' said Ida.

'That's true,' said Fa. 'But the one advantage we have over those chaps is money. We can afford fares and equipment that they probably can't.'

'That isn't fair,' said Ida.

'It isn't,' agreed Fa. 'Life seldom is fair.' He was quiet after that and Ida knew that he was thinking of Mama.

The rackety rhythm of the train on the track worked inside Ida's head. She thought of what Fa had told her: that six hundred Chinese coolies had died in the building of the thousand miles of track for this railway. The prairies were so flat wherever you looked that they made Ida feel as if she might fall off the Earth. She longed for walls or big trees to contain her. There were stations and townships that occasionally broke up that flatness. They saw Indians at one railroad station, standing holding horses, looking tall and dignified in their tasselled jackets and long black hair.

'I must write again to Grandmama and tell her about it all,' said Ida.

I have no address to put on this letter. We are on a railway train between Montreal and Vancouver (but they call it a railroad here).

28 August 1897

Dear Grandmama,
I hope that this letter finds you well.
Fa and I have seen an Indian lady, called a squaw, and she had a tiny brown baby tied to her back with a coloured blanket. The Indian mama had coloured beads threaded into the tassels of her leather tunic, rather like the beads that edge and weight those circles of linen you have on your jam jars when taking tea outside where there might be wasps. These beads were turquoise and red, and very lovely. That

Indian mama got up onto a spotted horse, with no saddle on its back, and she rode away with an Indian gentlemen and a girl who was younger, I think, than me. I thought how nice it would be to be an Indian baby carried everywhere by its mama, and then, when you are grown a little, to have a horse of your own to ride.

The country we see from this train is beyond anything I had imagined. We went over a bridge called Stoney Creek Bridge (a creek is what they call rivers here) over Rogers Pass, and we were so high above the gorge that I could feel panic almost stopping my breath! The gentlemen in our carriage laughed at me when they saw how I felt. For one moment I closed my eyes because I could not look at the drop below, knowing that our train would fall all that way if the bridge were to give way. Then I thought to myself how I will very likely never have occasion to see such a chasm ever again, and what a waste it would be to miss it after coming so far.

So, I did look out of the window after all, and felt a little faint at the sight, but it was wonderful to see. I had to try not to think how very heavy our train must be. It has a big engine at the front, of course. Then it has first class coaches, a restaurant car, sleeping cars, second class coaches, our gold rush coach, a mail car, and a baggage car. The whole must weigh a very great amount and the bridge appeared to be made of a webwork of metal that didn't look very strong at all. However, I am glad to report that we got to the other side quite safely.

We are into the Rocky Mountains now, rising up and down and over and through places. There are mountains with snow on the tops, pine trees and rushing brown rivers. It is a great effort for the engine to pull us all up the steeper slopes. We are told that a place called Big Hill has such a steep slope downwards that there have been trains run away on it, quite out of control, and the driver not able to stop or slow the train until the slope ran itself out. The highest place we reach is over five thousand feet above sea level. Fa says that sucking barley sugar sweets will help us prevent damage to our ears as the air pressure changes. I am sure that my geography studies are progressing far more thoroughly than if I had gone to St Margaret's School. But I do wish that I had studied sketching and painting as my cousins have, because then I would be able to show you some of these wonderful things. Fa is too occupied in his mind to find time to sketch what we see, which is a shame.

We are quite spoiled with girls coming offering refreshments from baskets, or boys selling newspapers for us to read. Fa and I have dined in the

*restaurant car on the train, and also at establishments
at stations, but I still find myself longing for cheese
on toast made with English cheese and eaten with
Cook's good chutney.*

*We pass through places with interesting names.
Eagle Pass sounds properly Indian, do you not think?
There is a place called Hope, which is a nice thought
for a name. I wonder what brought whoever named
it to give that particular name at that particular
time? I suspect they must have had a bad time of
things and were hoping that all would be well now
they were settled. There is also a Port Moody, which
sounds rather glum, although Fa says that he thinks
that place is probably named after a person with
the name Moody, rather than moodiness itself. Near
the end of our run we will come to Brighton and
Hastings, would you believe! What a pity we have
not brought our bathing clothes!*

*Fa says that he does not think that the postal
service will work in Alaska, so you must not worry if
you do not hear from us for some time. Meanwhile,
we are both well.*

With fondest regards,
Ida

Fa was too busy reading the Chicago Record's book and
making notes to notice much through the windows.

'There, Ida, I thought as much. There will be Chilkoot Indians eager to be engaged to carry luggage the twenty-eight miles from where we leave the boat to Lake Lindeman. Twenty-eight miles isn't so very far, especially if we don't have to carry the stuff ourselves.'

'And what happens once we are at that lake?' asked Ida.

'Then we make a boat. It says here that it takes four men one week to build a boat. Once we have a boat, we simply sail downstream when the ice melts. We must equip ourselves with a fast kind of boat if we are to beat others.'

Ida, reading over his shoulder, pointed out, 'It says there are "indescribably rough water rapids", so I hope that we will have a stable kind of a boat too!'

'Ah, yes, but there are Indian chaps who are happy to escort those who are too nervous to run the rapids on their own. Part way along we come to the town of Forty Mile, and that seems quite civilized with bakeries and restaurants and even an opera house.'

'Grandmama would be impressed!' said Ida.

'She would!' laughed Fa, his hands doing their excited dance. 'But we really mustn't get ahead of ourselves. First of all we must make absolutely sure to equip ourselves properly, or we will very soon be in trouble.'

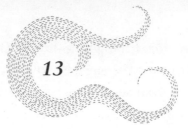

13

The seven-day train journey brought them into Vancouver, a busy city in which every building looked new, all of them along roads that were laid out in a grid. From there a smaller train took Fa and Ida and their luggage over the national boundary from Canada into America, to the bigger, older seaport of Seattle.

'Look!' said Ida, pointing to a large sign that stated, 'Gateway To The Gold Fields'. She felt her stomach surge with excitement, but also with fear. 'So, here we are,' said Fa, 'in the port that started the gold rush. Just think, Ida, up in the Klondike the men knew about the gold for months before news of it got out to the rest of the world. It wasn't until the ice melted and . . .'

'. . . a steamer could get down the Yukon River. I know, I know!' said Ida. 'The Portland steamer with its ton of gold packed into bags and boxes and pockets, and the prospectors, scruffy as tramps but rich as anything. I do know all that, Fa!' Ida crossed her arms. 'And one of those rich prospectors was a woman, remember! Tom Lippy and his wife carrying a suitcase between them that had more than two hundred pounds weight of gold in it.'

'And now it is our turn,' said Fa.

At the quay, funnels and masts and cranes' winches poked skywards above the big and small, smart and scruffy, boats and ships tied up to the wharf. Everywhere was a bustle of people, pushing and shouting, as they hurried about their buying of tickets and loading of goods onto ships.

'Look at that!' A horse was dangling from a sling as it was hoisted up and across, then down into the hold of a small steamboat.

'Goodness,' said Fa. 'All these people ahead of us! Maybe we shouldn't stop and buy goods here, after all? It does cost to transport goods, and perhaps we could buy what we need once we . . .'

'No, Fa!' Ida thumped him on the arm. 'You know very well that to buy anything at that Dyea place would cost many times what it will cost us here. Everyone has been saying so. They might not even have what we need.'

'But if it would get us ahead of the crowd . . . ?' Then Fa laughed. 'Gracious, you do look like your Grandmama when you are cross! But you are right, of course. It's just the thought of those already steaming upriver to the Yukon. And there are so very many here all heading to the Klondike.'

'In that case, let's hurry. Come on!'

They went up First Avenue and down Second Avenue looking at the numerous timber-built stores with their big signs and displays of goods outside them, all declaring that they were selling just what was needed for those setting off for the Klondike, yet selling quite different things.

'So confusing,' muttered Fa, pulling at his beard.

'Why do some of them spell Klondike with a C?' asked Ida.

'It is still so newly discovered,' said Fa, 'I suppose that nobody has set the spelling yet. Our doctor friend from the train told me that the name is actually the Thron-diuck River, and that Klondike is the Indian name mispronounced by the miners who've come back.'

Whatever goods the different stores had for sale, one thing they agreed about on their signs was that, however you spelled the name of the place, you were going to face extreme coldness and extreme remoteness from civilization.

Some recommended Indian buckskin jackets with tassels, with buckskin trousers and moccasins to match.

'How about . . . ?' began Fa.

'No!' said Ida, steering him away from that store.

Some sold great fur coats that came down to below the knee, with matching fur hats for the head.

'Far too bulky for ease of movement when climbing or boating,' said Fa. 'I have my good Harris tweed jacket, after all, which keeps out most weathers in my experience.'

But a store man persuaded Fa that he really did need a waterproof mackinaw raincoat to go on top, a woollen jumper to wear under his jacket and good winter shirts and underwear below even that. They also bought him thick woollen socks and a hat and gloves.

'I shall die of heatstroke!' said Fa.

Ida had her coat, but little else suited to such cold, so they bought her winter underwear, woollen skirts and a belted jacket, woollen stockings, blouses, a fur bonnet and gloves. Ida needed good strong boots to replace the shoes she was wearing. Cycling boots were recommended by the store man as being best for ladies. In fact, he tried to sell them bicycles too.

'Guaranteed to be the best way to get around once you're there,' he assured them. 'Faster than walking and no need to feed them as you would a horse.'

'But what about all our luggage?' asked Fa.

'Oh, I can sell you a trailer too; a trailer that'll convert to a sledge when you get to the snows, and convert again to a rocker for extracting the gold when the thaw comes.'

'Well, that sounds like a marvellous contraption!' said Fa.

'But it will cost more than we want to spend,' said Ida. 'Besides, there are mountains to be got over and rivers to be got down. How would we carry bicycles as well as everything else?'

Ida had to keep steering Fa away from items that promised to make the finding and extracting of gold easier. There was even a gold magnet.

'What a simple device!' said Fa. 'The simple ideas are always the best.'

'But gold isn't magnetic,' said Ida.

'Well, it's true that I hadn't thought that it was, but it surely must be, or how could they invent such a thing?' said Fa.

'It surely can't be, or why isn't everybody buying one?' countered Ida. Fa moved on to other implements, picking everything up, examining it and exclaiming over it. Steam-powered sleds, clockwork automated gold pans, x-ray machines that could 'see' gold.

'Food,' said Ida. 'That's what the book says we are really going to need, Fa. And rubber boots for standing in streams.'

They couldn't possibly carry all that they bought, so most of it was put into stiff canvas sacks, sewn up tight, with their Metcalf name painted onto the sides, then left stacked in a yard at the quay along with mountains of other prospectors' goods. Sacks and barrels and cases filled with flour, butter, evaporated potatoes and onions and apples, crystallized eggs, bacon, beans, coffee and tea, salt and sugar, raisins, yeast, dried fish, candles, soap, condensed milk, and more.

'I think these rules about taking a ton of goods have been invented by the store keepers who wish to sell all they can,' said Fa.

They bought cooking equipment – a collapsible metal stove, pans and cutlery. And mining equipment – pickaxes and shovels and buckets. A tent. And they needed to think about boats.

'What about one of these collapsible boats, eh, Ida?' said Fa, fingering the bundle of cut boards.

'What if it collapses when we are in it?' said Ida. 'And such a weight to carry!'

They added a saw and nails, and canvas for a sail, and decided to trust the lakeside trees to provide the wood that they would need.

'Such a quantity!' said Ida, looking at their pile of goods.

'It has all cost rather more than I was expecting.' Fa pulled at his beard. 'We must be careful with the money that we have left. I shall put aside the cost of travelling home and I won't touch that, whatever happens.'

There was a sign in the shop that stated that Alaska was the place where 'grub is more valuable than gold'. So why are we buying food in the hopes of getting gold, wondered Ida. It seemed a mad thing to be doing. But it must make sense or so many thousands would surely not leave their homes and risk their lives to do the same.

'We will find lots of gold,' declared Ida. 'And besides, we will have an adventure.'

Guest House, Seattle

28 August 1897

> *Dear Grandmama,*
> *I do hope that this letter finds you well. I am*

writing soon after my last letter because this may be the last chance we have to send any post for a long time. I send this from the town of Seattle. If you look on a map of America you will see it is on the west coast, just down from the line that divides Canada from America.

I wish that you could see the pile of supplies that we have ready for our trip. So many things and so much food that there is no danger at all of us going hungry once we arrive. Our Canadian government insists we take enough food to sustain someone for a whole year, if that should be necessary. So have no fear for us on that account.

I thought to tell you that I am not the only female prospector by any means. I think that above one in ten of those travelling are women, and very respectable women they are too. Such hats on display! Children as well, some a deal younger than I am, so the conditions in the Arctic cannot be so very severe.

Fa bought me a piece of golden nugget, would you believe? Not truly gold from the gold fields, but a kind of sweet treat they call candy here. It was made from peanuts and melted sugar, and it was quite delicious.

I think of England, and of you, and I hope that you are now happily settled into the Dower House. Are you in Mama and Papa's bedroom?

I think of Mama often. I feel that she would be cheering Fa and me on our way. I do hope so. She did so enjoy adventures in books.

We are to board our steamship this afternoon. We have tickets from the Alaska Steamship Company. Fa has booked us a cabin, and we are promised 'first-class meals for all', so we shall be entirely comfortable on our voyage.

Did you know that gold is the most malleable of all metals? It can be beaten to become gold leaf that is four hundred times thinner than a hair from your head. Is that not astonishing? Gold is nineteen times heavier than water and seven times heavier than quartz stone. You see, I am learning science as well as geography on this trip. Do tell Cook that I seem fit to learn a great deal about cookery too, once we are off this ship and no longer being cared for by others.

Your loving granddaughter,
Ida

14

The steamship from Seattle to Dyea was not as 'entirely comfortable' as they had been led to believe. Fa paid twenty dollars for their two tons of luggage to be stowed aboard. He paid forty dollars for a cabin for Ida and himself. But there was no cabin. There were just hard rough bunks against a wall, freshly made of splintery pine planks, and a curtain hung by way of a screen.

'They've gutted the blessed boat and crammed in as many berths as possible!' said Fa in disgust. 'Treating us as if we were cattle going to market in order to maximise their takings, with no thought at all for passenger comfort!'

'There's rain dripping down from above,' said Ida, wiping a drop from her face. But it wasn't raining outside. They soon worked out that what was dripping was horse urine, soaking through the boards from where horses were crated on the deck above.

'Disgraceful!' declared Fa. 'I shall complain to the steward!' But there was no steward on this ship, and it was soon clear that there was little point in complaining about anything since nothing could be done to change things now.

'Unless you'd like to step back ashore?' said somebody hopefully. 'There's plenty as would like to take your place!'

'No thank you,' said Fa. 'We shall stick it out. But it isn't right, you know!'

Despite all that, there was a small feeling of triumph as the overladen old steamboat laboured away from its mooring and rolled out into open sea. Ida stood in the crowd of travellers who thronged the deck, waving hands and hats, even climbing onto cabin roofs and up rigging to make more of a show of their farewell to their old lives. And those on the quay waved and wept to loved ones they hoped to see returning with fortunes in the months to come. Now that they were amongst people who had all left family behind, having no Mama felt strangely normal. Ida just ached with wishing that there could be Mama to come back home to once their adventure was complete.

The ship had been called a schooner on the poster but it was actually a rough little steamboat, and life aboard was bad. They soon found that another three men and one whole family with small children had been sold the same 'cabin' as Fa. They all tried sleeping in turns, rigging up a canvas sheet to keep the horse pee off the top sleeper. But Ida found it more comfortable in the end to bed down on the bales of hay being stored for horse feed. Fa and others soon joined her in that dark dank corner.

'I don't like to have been cheated again,' grumbled Fa, up on deck, away from the stink for a while.

'Quite right, Sir!' said a gentleman in a dog collar. 'We must attempt to keep up standards, whatever the circumstances. I tell you, there are people set on swindling any newcomer to Alaska. We must all be on our guard.'

'We must,' agreed Fa. 'Are you hunting for gold yourself, Sir?'

'No,' the gentleman assured him. 'Hunting for souls would be nearer to the truth. Let me introduce myself. The Reverend Charles Bowers.'

'Frank Metcalf. And my daughter, Ida.' Fa shook the man's hand, and Ida too took the gentleman's big strong hand as he smiled down at her.

'Charming!' he said. 'Tell me, Mr Metcalf, do you have your money in a safe place? I'm told there are pickpockets aboard this very ship.' The Reverend Bowers whispered, 'Is your cash about your person? Perhaps in a vulnerable pocket?'

Fa patted his chest at the place where the inner pocket held his wallet of notes.

'Fa!' said Ida, but the Reverend Bowers laughed at her.

'What? Do you mistrust a man of the church?'

Ida blushed. She didn't like him.

'A sound plan, but do take care,' said the Reverend Bowers. 'This is a return journey for me. I have been visiting my family, but am now returning to my flock, some of whom are not good men, I'm sorry to say. Beware of the crooks you will meet along the way, Mr Metcalf. It is all too easy to be conned if one doesn't know better.' He paused, then raised a finger. 'Mr Metcalf, I could introduce you to the very best people to help with your packing and portage?'

'Oh, how very kind of you!' said Fa, his face open with delight. 'Why, that will certainly be of great help. Thank you!'

'Not at all,' said the Reverend Bowers, and his mouth smiled, but his eyes had already slithered away and across to focus on somebody else.

Fa hugged Ida to him. 'Well, that is a bit of luck! To have met such a man in such a place. So kind. I fancy that he was offering kindness to us because I had a child with me. You are proving to be my lucky charm, Ida! We shall do very well on this trip.'

The sea voyage up the west coast was far less comfortable than their trip across the Atlantic Ocean had been, but it was much shorter. The dining room soon became a kind of dormitory where people slept and lived. The 'first-class meals' were few in number and decidedly not first class in quality. The food that was cooked in the galley was brought out on trays. Ida and Fa learned to follow the example of others and simply grab bowls of soup and hunks of bread from those trays as they passed by.

'For what we are about to receive!' laughed the Reverend Bowers, also helping himself.

'May the Lord make us truly thankful!' finished Fa. 'And, do you know, I truly am thankful for anything to eat by the time this arrives!' It was such a relief to see

Fa able to joke in such conditions, that Ida truly was thankful too.

There was rough weather and driving rain out at sea. The horses stamped and panicked. A crate of dogs was washed overboard. The hundreds of people crowded into the ship were all prone to seasickness. The stench was abominable, the place cold and leaky and unstable.

'But we are getting there,' said Fa, holding a handkerchief to his nose. 'Just think of gold!' Ida tried to think of the gold, but it didn't make her feel any warmer.

It took four days to reach Dyea, the last part of the voyage being up an inlet, away from the rough seas and into a calmer place with land either side. The ninety-mile long Lynn Canal had huge, magnificent mountains either side of it, all reflected in the turquoise water.

'Are those the mountains we must cross?' asked Ida.

'I suppose they must be. Gosh, those poor people trying to travel with bicycles!' said Ida.

'There,' said Fa. 'The numbers of those competing with us are dropping already.'

Huddled against the chill, Ida and Fa leaned together on the ship's rail as they passed the town of Skagway with its board buildings and mass of dirty white tents.

'That town is a place to keep well clear of,' said the Reverend Bowers, who was suddenly at their side once more. 'You do well to land at Dyea. Altogether a better kind of place, but still one with dangers for the unwary tenderfoot.'

'What is so wrong with Skagway?' asked Ida.

'Oh, shootings and lawlessness of all sorts,' said the Reverend Bowers. 'Trickery and wickedness. Why, there's a telegraph office in the main street where you can pay five dollars to send a wire to your family anywhere in the world.'

'That's a good thing, surely?' said Ida.

'No,' said the Reverend Bowers. 'It's a truly bad thing because there is no telegraph line linking that place to anywhere at all. It's all a stealing operation, a scam. You'd be surprised at the number who fall for it. There's any number of ways they'll take the gold from a man who's mined it, or money from the man who is on his way to the gold. Why, I almost admire the ingenuity of those criminal minds!'

'The sooner we are onto the mountain trail the better,' muttered Fa.

'I've not forgotten my promise,' said the Reverend Bowers. 'I'll find you the best men I know to help with your luggage. A business calling itself the Reliable Packers is the one I'd recommend. I can vouch it calls itself that name for a reason.'

'Then I must give you a donation for your church mission in return for your kindness,' said Fa, reaching into his jacket.

'Oh, no need for that!' said the Reverend Bowers. Fa's hand was already slipping under his coat so that he could fetch out his wallet, but the Reverend Bowers laid a hand on his arm to stop him. 'I don't offer my service in the hope of reward in this world. Please keep your money. You will have need of it.'

'There's another place full of tents!' said Ida. 'Is that one Dyea?' The mass of white tents looked almost like snow covering the bottom of the valley up ahead of them.

The boat's engines shuddered and stopped. For a moment, the people on board went quiet, then they began grabbing for their bundles of luggage.

'But we are still in midwater!' said Ida. 'Is there no wharf?'

An anchor was dropped into the water with a splash. They were a mile or so from shore, and that shore was a shallow muddy beach. No gangplanks, no cranes to lift goods, no porters.

'I really don't . . .' began Fa as he was pushed aside by people dropping their goods over the side of the boat.

'Look!' said Ida, pointing. There were flat rafts being paddled from the beach towards the steamer, and rowing boats too. But some of the people on the steamer weren't waiting for any form of transport. They simply went over the side of the boat and waded ashore through the seawater, their bundles held aloft.

'It must be so cold in that water!' said Ida. 'Do we have to . . .'

'Absolutely not!' There was the Reverend Bowers,

appearing again so suddenly he made Ida jump. 'Follow me!' He shoved his way through the throng of people, ushering Fa and Ida to where a ladder hung down the side of the steamer and a man in a rowing boat waited at the bottom. 'This here's my friend who will row you two good people to the beach. His men will collect your luggage, for a small fee of course, and you will be reunited with it on the beach. I imagine that it is all labelled?'

'Oh, yes,' assured Fa. 'All in canvas bundles marked Metcalf.'

'Hear that, Hank?' shouted the Reverend Bowers to the man on the raft. 'You look after my friend Mr Metcalf and his daughter, you hear me? Give them your best service.'

As the rowing boat pushed away from the big boat, and Hank rowed them towards the sand, Fa wiped a hand over his brow. 'Goodness, what a scrum! And what luck to have had help.'

Soon Fa and Ida were standing on the beach, their feet sinking into the salty cold water that saturated the sands. They watched the steamer being unloaded in astonishment. Hank had rowed back out to fetch more people to land. There were people and belongings everywhere, and a frantic feel in the air.

'The poor horses!' said Ida. The horses were being lowered over the side of the steamer one at a time and plunged into the icy seawater where they thrashed their way towards land.

'Look! Oh, dear!' A horse had panicked and moved, just as somebody's bags were being dropped overboard to be put onto a raft. With a splash, the bags were in the water and men were whipping the horse.

'The bags have gone down!' said Ida.

'What a waste of whatever was in those bundles.'

'But it wasn't the horse's fault!' said Ida.

Fa shook his head. 'I do hope that all of our stuff is secure, having got it so far. How many bundles did we have in all, Ida? Do you remember?'

'I don't know,' said Ida.

'Nor do I,' said Fa. He tugged at his beard and said no more.

We must learn to look after our stuff, or it'll soon be gone, thought Ida. And in that big surging crowd of people on the beach, she suddenly felt very alone.

Dogs and goats and horses, boxes and trunks and duffle bags and sacks and crates were all unloaded onto the beach. Fa and Ida walked along the beach and back, looking for the Metcalf name. Some of the luggage had burst open as it was thrown around. There were sacks of flour and dried vegetables sinking into the wetness.

'Tide's coming in!' somebody shouted. 'Get it all moved!' And suddenly the flurry was less from the boat to the beach and more from the beach to above the high-tide mark.

'But where in Heaven's name is our man?' asked Fa.

'Where is our stuff?' Fa's hands were beginning to do the flustered flappy dance that Ida recognised so well from whenever he got alarmed.

'I think he's there,' said Ida, pointing. 'The man in the red chequered shirt.'

'Ah, yes. You stay here on the dry,' Fa told Ida. 'I'll sort it all out.' He started to wade through a puddle on the sands to where a stack of Metcalf luggage was at last being piled.

'Thank you,' said Fa. 'Now, how much do I owe you chaps for your services?' Ida didn't hear their reply, but she heard Fa's exclaimed, 'Good Lord, that's a vast sum for a couple of hours' work!' Fa mentioned the reverend gentleman, to which there was a mutter of reply and some laughter. Then one of the men began taking bundles off the pile, as if to send them back out to the steamer moored in the inlet. Fa's hands were instantly dancing again.

'No, no! Leave them be. I shall pay you, of course. But I am not happy!' The men didn't look the least bit concerned that Fa wasn't happy. They held out their hands, which Fa piled with notes. He came back to Ida, his shoulders drooping.

'Oh, my dear Ida, whatever sort of place have I brought you to?'

'The Reverend Bowers tricked us?' said Ida.

Fa nodded. 'Gulled me completely! Those chaps charged me a small fortune. On top of that, it's strange, but there don't appear to be the number of notes left in my wallet that I had thought were there.' Fa shook his head. 'But a man of the church would surely not . . .'

'Are you talking of that Reverend Bowers?' asked a man with a face as wrinkled and brown as a walnut.

'I was,' said Fa. 'Do you know the fellow?

'Know of him,' said the man. 'That money of yours is gone, my friend. There's no point in chasing it because you won't get it back. Reverend Bowers is one of Soapy Smith's gang of thieves from Skagway. Actors and thieves, every one of them.'

Fa looked utterly lost. Ida shook his arm.

'Fa! We must move our stuff to somewhere safe. Then find a place to sleep. Come on, Fa! We must save all those expensive goods that we bought.' Ida stomped over to the mountain of bundles labelled with their Metcalf name and heaved one of them onto her shoulders. She headed up the beach towards the shanty and tent town, with no idea at all where she was going. To her relief, Fa followed, carrying his big leather case over the wet muddy sand. Thank goodness Fa isn't here on his own, thought Ida. Food revived Fa. The meal of chewy bacon and beans supplied by the rough little shack that called itself a hotel didn't taste good, but it was warm and filling.

'Prices one might pay in a top London hotel,' said Fa, poking a bent fork around the lumps in his bowl. 'The meals that we shall buy once we've made our fortune will no doubt taste all the sweeter for being in contrast to this.'

Ida thought of all that good food from the kitchen at the big house. And the bedroom she might have had there, all to herself, with a feather mattress and a maid to bring hot water for washing and . . .

'You fresh off that boat?' asked a man with desperate eyes peering from a shaggy grey mass of hair and beard.

'We are,' said Fa.

'Well, get yourself right back where you came from as quick as you can,' said the man. 'You won't believe what you'll find on that trail, Mister. With winter coming it's going to get nothing but worse. Why, they tell me that soon there'll be no sunlight to speak of, night or day. That's a kind of Hell on earth, before you even reckon in temperatures too cold for a man to survive in the normal way of things. No gold's worth killing yourself for by my reckoning. I'm off home, back to my family, and I don't care if they think me a fool for not bringing back so much as one speck of gold.'

'Goodness!' said Fa.

The man's boots were worn to tatters and his clothes dirty and ragged. He's tried hard before giving up, Ida realised, and she felt fear chilling her insides.

Then a couple of men, almost black-faced from sunshine and dirt, burst into the hotel dining room. They carried small bags slung from their belts, and those bags looked heavy. The men were singing, 'Oh, there's plenty of gold, so I've been told . . .'

'. . . on the banks of the Sacramento!' finished Ida. 'But the Sacramento is in California!'

''Tis too, pretty lady!' laughed one of the men. 'But there's plenty of gold in the Klondike too. We've got our share and we're on out of here. Home for Christmas!'

'See?' said Fa, his eyes sparkling at Ida. 'It can be done! And with so many heading for home, there'll be all the more gold for us!' Fa suddenly threw his hat into the air as if he was a cowboy. 'Yeeee-ha!' he shouted.

'Shush, Fa!' said Ida, trying to pull his arms down. But it was nice to see him happy.

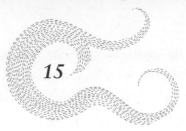

15

There was a choice of two routes over the mountains. The Chicago Record's book said that the White Pass was lower and gentler than the Chilkoot Pass.

'And you can take packhorses on the White Pass,' Ida told Fa. But,

'No,' said Fa, and soon Ida overheard talk that explained Fa's response.

'Hardly one horse survives that trail. Corpses of the poor creatures left, right, in front and behind you, all stinking to high heaven, enough to make a strong man sick to the stomach.'

Ida and Fa went to find Indian porters to carry all their goods up and over the Chilkoot Pass to the lakes.

'It will take more than one trip to carry everything,' said Fa. 'But it is only twenty-eight miles and these Indian chaps are as strong as anything.

But the 'chaps' weren't all chaps. There were Indian women and children too, and Ida watched them all in fascination at the weighing and packing station. The women and the bigger children carried huge packs on their backs, alongside the men. They had high cheekbones and straight jet-black hair and dark eyes. Most of the men had long droopy moustaches. The adults had noses the shape of eagle beaks, and a look as haughty as eagles too.

There were other people at the packing station who had come off the same boat as Fa and Ida. The crowd jostled and shouted, bargaining prices and loads.

'There doesn't appear to be any kind of a queue,' said Fa, dithering on the edge of the scrum. Some Indian women had a stall selling moccasins and parka coats with fur linings, and strange looking foodstuffs. Ida's cycling boots were still wet from yesterday, wet and tight and cold on her feet. The loose leather moccasins looked soft and inviting. Ida reached out a finger to touch one.

'Too much big,' said the woman. She indicated that her daughter, sitting stitching, could make some that would be the right size for Ida.

'Come along, Ida,' said Fa, heading towards the porters. But the Indian woman held Ida's coat sleeve and pointed.

'Take. For mountain,' she said, pointing to a pile of shrivelled brown bits.

'What is it?' asked Ida. The brown stuff looked the kind of thing that a witch might throw into a potion.

'Make tea,' said the woman. 'Up mountain, ill.' She mimed somebody stumbling and sick. 'Take tea – better.'

'Really?' said Ida. 'But we already have a medicine chest with iodine and bandages and . . .'

'Not good!' The woman was insistent, shaking her head. 'Need.' The woman was fierce and Ida began to feel scared.

'But I'm afraid that I haven't any money. I will ask my father,' said Ida, looking over to see that Fa was now in the thick of the throng around a weighing machine.

'This!' said the woman. She pointed to a button on Ida's coat.

'But I need that to do my coat . . . Oh!' Ida gasped, as a little knife was suddenly in the woman's hand and, quick as a fish, it had sliced through the stitching at Ida's chest and the woman had taken the blue button. Ida was trembling now, stumbling back, and about to run away. But the woman caught Ida's hand and, even as Ida tried to snatch her hand away, the woman pressed a paper-wrapped parcel into it.

'Good medicine tea,' she insisted.

'Oh, yes,' said Ida, then she fled.

'Fa!' Ida grabbed at his arm.

'I have a couple of porters,' said Fa. 'A man and a woman. They will carry everything, although they're charging an extortionate price for it.'

Other prospectors, some with faces and fists tight with anger, were turning away from the porters' station. Fa bent to whisper to Ida, 'Actually, these high price might be a blessing in disguise.'

'How?'

'Well, this is going to slow down those who can't afford them. Don't look at me like that, Ida. This is a race!'

They began the trek the next day, setting off along the

Dyea Valley. Ida's smooth-soled boots slipped on the muddy track, but she didn't complain. Fa was puffing along with a pack strapped to his back and the Indian man and woman porters were carrying huge packs hanging from straps that they braced across their foreheads. Ida simply carried a satchel bag slung across her body.

'Shouldn't I carry more?' she asked.

'Certainly not,' said Fa. 'What would Grandmama think if I treated you like a pack mule?'

So Ida rather enjoyed the walk to begin with. The sun showed itself briefly and there was excited chatter amongst the crowd of walkers starting out. Some walked beside packhorses piled with their luggage. Others had carts that would only be of use on these early, flatter, parts of the trek. One of the carts was pulled by goats. Many of the male prospectors carried their own goods, backs bent under the weight of boxes or sacks. Others, like Fa and Ida, were using Indian porters, who very soon disappeared, walking far faster than them in spite of the great weights they were carrying.

It was interesting seeing what people were choosing to take to such a remote part of the world. Ida spotted a rocking chair and even a piano. She supposed that it would be pleasant to have those things when setting up a new home in the Klondike. She slipped into a happy daydream of how she would furnish a little house for herself and Fa. She could make seats from logs and put flowers in jam jars, just as she and her friend Minnie used to do when they made dens in the wood back at home in Norfolk.

The cart track wandered by and over the river, through the rustling shelter of cottonwood trees and birch and willow. Ida thought of the beach back at home. She thought of Mama walking over the clacking pebbles in her properly buttoned boots and billowing skirts, stooping and picking up a pebble to roll between her fingers. She remembered paddling her bare feet in the sparkling shallows whilst Mama said something, laughing, that was blown away on the wind. Ida sighed.

As the day wore on, the muddy trail between steep valley sides led on to a track through woodland. Tree stumps and roots were tangled in the slick mud to trip and bruise you if you weren't concentrating on every footstep, especially if you had no grip on your boots. Ida felt the weight of her bag cutting into her shoulder as it swayed with each step. She was very glad that Fa had not let her carry anything heavier. Others were abandoning things on the side of the track. A bag of sugar. A wooden crate, nailed shut. The piano.

'You can go faster with a lighter load,' said Fa. 'I am beginning to wonder whether we truly need all that we have brought with us.'

'But every bit of it was on that list,' said Ida. 'They won't let us over the border unless we have the full ton of outfit each.'

Actually, they had at least two items that weren't on the official list. Ida had her Duffle dog. Mama had made Duffle when Ida had measles when she was six. She had sat at her bedside and stitched him out of one of Fa's old brown socks, all whilst telling stories about him, every day until Ida was better. The other thing that wasn't on the list was a photograph of Mama in a frame that Ida had seen was in Fa's bag.

They came to a settlement by a river crossing, Finnegan's Point, with a wooden saloon selling whisky, and a blacksmith's shop and a mass of tents. Some stopped to rest or camp here, but Ida and Fa kept going, following their porters who were nowhere in sight. Over a bridge on to a track full of boulders and tree roots, on through woods to another camp.

'Pleasant Camp,' said Fa.

'Could we . . . ?' began Ida.

'Better keep going,' said Fa. 'The porters have carried on.' But Fa did pause long enough to take a paper twist full of raisins out of his pack. Ida was glad to share them, but the brief stop made it hard to start walking again. Her feet were sore, her legs ached, and she could see by the droop of Fa's shoulders that he was struggling too.

The path headed uphill now, and Ida's legs felt the strain of every step. They climbed up through woodland then, at last, burst out from the trees, where, 'Gracious!' said Ida.

There in front of them was a massive encampment of

tents, on the margin between woodland and bare rock that rose up into mountains.

'This must be Sheep Camp,' said Fa, straightening up and putting a hand up to shade his eyes as he looked around and up at the mountains walling the valley head.

'Do we . . . ?' began Ida, fingers crossed within her mittens.

'We do stop here,' said Fa. 'Yes. See? There are our porters.' He lifted the satchel over Ida's head, leaving her feeling so suddenly light that it was almost like floating.

The porters had already set up Fa and Ida's tent for them.

'Just as well,' said Fa. For the sky was darkening and the air chilling enough to start to freeze the muddy ground.

'Where will the Indians sleep?' whispered Ida. There wasn't enough room for more than two in their tent and the porters hadn't taken any luggage of their own.

'I understand there is some kind of a wooden shack where all the porters sleep and eat together,' said Fa.

There were hundreds of tents, many of them as crisp and clean as the Metcalf one. Beside those tents were mounds of grubby grey and brown bundles of goods, each mound marked with a name on a stake. The Metcalf pile seemed very small compared with others. Ida's feet throbbed and she could feel painful blisters where her boots had rubbed.

'There must be above a thousand people here,' said Fa in wonder.

Ida and Fa sat, exhausted, on their bundles, just looking around at the towering mountains and the mass of people and tents and luggage, as dusk fell. It was all very strange.

Some people had thrown together piles of branches brought from the woods to make fires that began to spark and flare into the blackness of the night. Ida was glad to warm herself, although the fire burned her face while leaving her back freezing cold.

'How will we keep warm when we go up where there aren't any trees?' asked Ida.

'I'm told that there is timber one can buy up there,' said Fa. 'But at a price. Only fair, I suppose, since it all has to be hauled up.'

It seemed that everything was 'at a price', and a stiff price at that. Among the shacks and tents there were places where women and men had set up kitchens and were selling food. The smell of hot bacon and beans made Ida's mouth water.

'We must cook for ourselves as a rule,' said Fa. 'But tonight our stove is still in Dyea, so we will buy a hot meal.'

Full on beans and bacon and coffee, Ida and Fa settled in their tent, bundled in blankets on the rubber ground sheet. There was no chance to wash or clean teeth or change into nightclothes. Ida pulled her coat on top of her blanket, trying to find more warmth. The rubber and new canvas was smelly. From outside came the sound of howling dogs, and people arguing or singing or stumbling about. Flickering light and shadow-shapes danced menacingly over the tent walls. Fa reached out a hand and stroked Ida's hair.

'You did well today, my love. Very well. Now, shall we pray for Mama and Grandmama and Uncle Stephen and your cousins and our friends back in England? And pray too for our own safety and good fortune.'

Ida closed her eyes tight and prayed very hard indeed.

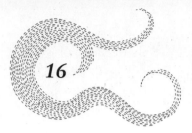

16

They awoke to the sound of people shouting, horses being harnessed, and the smell of bacon frying. Fa leapt from his blanket bundle, hair on end, arms flying.

'Quick, Ida, or we shall be left behind! Can you look for that bundle of flapjack that I packed into your satchel bag? That will have to do for our breakfast.'

The porters had a fire going with a burned-black pot of coffee hung over it. The woman porter handed Fa and Ida a steaming tin mug each.

'Thank you very much,' said Ida. The coffee was bitter, with no milk, but Ida was glad of it. As she stood and drank she looked up at the thin track leading on to the mountains, already solid with climbers inching upwards. It was as if gold really was magnetic after all, pulling them all up into the clouds, thought Ida. But she and Fa couldn't begin that climb yet. First they had to bring the rest of their stuff up from Dyea to Sheep Camp.

'Look at the sky,' said Fa. 'I think we're in for rain.'

As they tied the tent shut and set off back down the track towards Dyea, the rain started. And soon it turned to snow. The porters set off at a fast rate. Ida and Fa did their best to hurry along the crowded path after them.

That stumbling and muddy, tree-rooted track down to Dyea and back became very familiar over the following days. Down and up, down and up, lifting and lugging heavy wet canvas-wrapped packs of food and equipment, reducing the mountain of Metcalf goods in Dyea and building a new mountain of Metcalf goods at Sheep Camp. The Indian porter man carried almost twice what Fa carried. Fa and the lady porter carried a similar weight, but the lady went faster. Ida managed one small pack.

'Remarkable people, these Indians,' panted Fa, as he struggled, bent over under the hundred-pound case he had strapped to his back. 'They put a fellow to shame.' They put a girl even more to shame, thought Ida. I am slowing Fa down and making him have to pay more for porters than he would if he was on his own. The porters' rates of pay went up almost by the day as more and more people wanted to employ them. Fa grimly paid up.

'If we scrimp now, we will be beaten to the best pickings of gold. That would be a false economy,' he said. 'Paying for speed is an investment.' But only if we really do find enough gold when we get there, thought Ida.

The porters refused to work on Sundays, and it wasn't just them who stopped still that one day of the week. Nobody liked to tempt fate by failing to respect the Lord's Day, and besides, everyone needed the rest.

'I didn't used to like Sundays at the big house,' said Ida. 'It was dull. But I like Sundays here.' It was such a relief to stop for a few hours, to sleep for longer, to take more care over cooking, to repair things, and to simply be still.

'Just one more day to bring up the last of our goods from Dyea,' said Fa, rubbing his hands over the fire. 'And then we turn and face the mountains at last.'

'Could we send a letter to Grandmama?' asked Ida.

'Certainly,' said Fa. 'But it might not leave Dyea for a few months. The sea is beginning to freeze up, so the last boat of the year may already have gone.'

So, that Sunday afternoon, Ida unpacked the beautiful pen from its wrappings deep inside her clothes bag, where it was kept safe from freezing. She found some paper – only a torn, paper flour bag, light brown in colour – wrapped herself in two blankets, placed the crumpled paper on the flat lid of a tin, beside a couple of lit candles, flattened it with her hand and began to write:

Sheep Camp

A Sunday, I think in November, but we have rather lost track of dates

Dear Grandmama,
I hope that you are properly well. I am sorry to be sending you a letter on such rough paper, but we don't have any finer paper to hand. We are, at present, living in a town of tents at the base of some

very large mountains, so large that I have only seen the tops once, when the clouds moved clear of them just for a moment. The day after tomorrow, Fa and I will climb up those mountains and go up into the clouds. I shall feel like Jack from 'Jack and the Beanstalk'. Jack was after gold, just as we are. Might I find a giant up there? Or a goose laying golden eggs? I will let you know once we are safely down the other side, but that will not be for a long time, not, perhaps, until next year, Fa says.

It being Sunday, there is no work today. You will be glad to hear that people of all kinds keep Sundays, even our Indian porters. Fa says they are strict Presbyterians, but they have some different beliefs from the chapel people I know from home. When they eat meat or use leather they thank the spirit of the creature which has fed or clothed them. I feel that is a good thing to do, don't you? There are church services held in the open here, often under sky that is snowing on us. The singing is a little rough, but I like it, especially when a man plays his fiddle to the hymns.

You would find it strange living in a tent, but Fa and I are quite used to it now. Fa can never sit up straight, him being so tall and the tent so low. I am thankful that I am short. Last night a stray horse put a hoof through the canvas, giving us quite a fright. There are sad horses loose all around the camp as their owners leave them when they head up the mountain trail. That trail is so steep one couldn't possibly get a horse up it, or almost any other animal, although I have seen a man with a dog strapped to his back setting off that way. Some dogs have no food and no shelter when their owners have moved on without them. They howl through the night, sounding terribly mournful. Fa says we cannot feed or help them because we too must move on and we haven't enough to spare.

You might tell Tilly that I have been stitching, just the way that she taught me to, but with coarse thread and a large fat needle, using a block of wood to push the needle through the canvas, as I try to repair the tear in the tent. Even though it is snowing outside, inside we are cosy in a dim kind of way. The snow on the tent helps shelter us from the winds. Our days are very short, and getting shorter as the nights lengthen. Soon the days will almost disappear altogether, which will be strange. This is a black and white world of snow and rocks and bare trees and white tents, and I do long for the spring when we shall see green again.

Before spring we must move all our goods over the mountains to the lakes where we will await the thaw to open the river route to the Yukon. That feels a long way off in time, just as you feel a long way off in distance. Strangely, Mama feels quite close to us here. I know very well that she would smile her small smile and say, 'Gracious, Ida!' if she could see me in my fur cap! And she would frown her small frown at Fa and say, 'Do be careful, Frank' if she could see the size of the loads that he carries on his back. She is very probably with you too, Grandmama, shaking her head and saying 'Aren't they a worry to us?' but you have no need to worry. We are well able and well equipped for the excitements that lie ahead.

Your loving granddaughter,
Ida

As Ida carefully wrapped and packed the pen once more, she wondered quite how many weeks or months it would be before she found occasion to use it again.

'Are you ready for more beans, Fa? Shall I fry some bacon to go with them?'

Fa made a face. 'I'd give my father's gold pocket watch for a bowl of fresh vegetables rather than blessed beans again. Or a nice fresh fish. How about one of Jim's fresh-caught mackerel, cooked with butter and parsley and a squeeze of lemon. With a hunk of bread still warm from the oven, and salad on a side dish!' Jim was Minnie's father and an expert fisherman.

'I'm sorry,' said Ida. 'It's bacon and beans or nothing.

I've been soaking a whole bucket of beans ready.' Fa raised his eyebrows when he saw the quantity of beans, but Ida explained. 'I'll do them with molasses and mustard powder to give them some taste.' A man in a neighbouring tent had shown her how to cook them that way. 'And I'll make a big quantity so that we have food waiting when we've done the mountain climb tomorrow, and for a few days after.'

'Excellent idea,' smiled Fa. And Ida felt a little as though she was, at least sometimes, more help than hindrance to him, and that was a relief.

17

Two days later they began the steep climb up the mountain pass.

'Four miles to the top,' said Fa. But those four miles were so steep that a man might be on hands and knees in parts and still be almost upright. This was the Chilkoot Pass.

Fa lifted Ida's pack onto her back. Even when she was standing still, she felt the weight dragging at her. Fa strapped a large crate to his own back, then took a canvas bundle in his arms as well. Ida stamped her cold feet to try and get the feeling back into them. She wrapped her woollen scarf around her lower face, it was beginning to go numb with the cold. Lucky Fa having a beard, she thought.

The mountain ahead was white with snow, rearing up and butting into the clouds. Up that distant white mountain ran a black trail of people reaching from Sheep Camp into those clouds. It looked like a black dribble of molasses down a tin. Every man and woman doing the climb was bent over by the weight of what they carried. Like the pictures in Grandmama's Bible of people going down to Hell weighed down by the burden of their sins, thought Ida. Only going up instead of down.

'Ready?' said Fa. Ida nodded. They began the climb, joining the line of people step-shuffling, prodding sticks and taking steps in a rhythm that none could break without halting the whole line. Step, step, step. Fa's booted feet were in front of Ida's, and another pair of feet were close behind her. Ida tried to step-step steadily in the men's rhythm, but her steps were shorter than theirs. She had to dance the odd double-step to catch up, and that took extra breath, winding her slightly each time she did it, especially as the path began to steepen. Ida's smooth leather soles slipped, making her slide backwards into the man behind. He was kind at first, but he soon became cross as exhaustion shortened all their tempers.

'This ain't no place for a gal!' he said, more than once. 'What in tarnation is that Englishman thinking of, bringing a gal to this?'

Ida wanted to say something short and sharp and clever back to the man, but she could think of no suitable reply. She hadn't the breath to spare anyway. It took all her energy just to put one foot in front of the other, up and up and up. Ida counted steps. She sang songs in her head to the rhythm of the steps. 'Molly Malone' was one she'd sung at school in Norfolk, and there were hymns she had learned in church, some of them with military marching tunes. All kept her head busy and her feet plodding and her breath panting in time with it all.

Every so often the line would stop, and the shout would

go out, 'Hold up!' Then they'd all kick their feet into the snow to get a good foothold and stop for however long it took for whatever the problem ahead was to sort itself out. It felt so good to break that rhythm and rest! And yet Ida grew to dread the call to halt because her sweat swiftly chilled into a clammy coldness that made her feel sick. Her legs felt strangely weak and wobbly whenever she stopped, and she was frightened that they might not work properly when she asked them to climb again. The effort of re-starting the climb began to make her groan out loud each time. She wasn't the only one. It was strange walking as one of so many, mostly in silence save for the regular plod of feet and the occasional moan or groan. We sound like ghouls, she thought.

They stopped properly at a ledge of land big enough for tents and piles of goods and food stalls, and a mass of resting climbers. That place was called Scales.

'Called that because the porters are going to weigh the goods again,' panted Fa. 'Lord knows why. They'll weigh the same as they did at the bottom of the climb.'

Fa and Ida's two porters were waiting for them as they got to Scales. They stood amongst a group of Indians, their mittened hands warming around steaming mugs of coffee. The sight of that hot steam and the smell of the coffee made Ida's mouth water. You could buy hot drinks and doughnuts from a stall, but she saw from the sign that the price for a drink and doughnut was two dollars and fifty cents, the same price as the fine three-course meal in Seattle had cost. So Ida looked away and tried not to want them as much as she did.

The man porter stepped forward as Fa and Ida took off their own packs to ease their backs. He said something to Fa that Ida didn't hear, but:

'A dollar for every pound of weight?' said Fa, arms flailing. 'Certainly not! We had an agreed price and, as a gentleman, I expect you to honour that agreement, just as I shall myself.'

'No pay, no carry,' said the porter. He folded his arms and glared back at Fa.

'Scoundrels!' muttered Fa.

'Shush, Fa!' said Ida. People were looking.

'We're all hit the same as you,' said one man, taking off his hat and scratching his head. 'They all put up their prices jist here, I'm told. It don't bother them none if you say you won't pay 'cos there's plenty more coming along behind who are willing to pay whatever sum they care to dream up.'

Ida looked down the slope at the hundreds, probably thousands, of people pouring upwards in a never-ending trail, each of them eager to shift their ton of goods up the mountain, pack by pack, as fast as possible.

'Well I must say that I don't like it!' said Fa. But he reached into a pocket deep inside his coat and paid the extra, all in coins. The Indians didn't trust paper money.

'At least your pockets will be lighter for the rest of the climb,' said Ida.

'Hmm,' said Fa.

'Can we have something to eat, and then the packs will be lighter still?' asked Ida.

So they ate more flapjacks and handfuls of raisins, and drank melted snow water from the corked bottle they'd brought. Ida felt as though she was drinking icicles. She could feel the freezing cold of it travelling down her middle.

'Shall we share a coffee?' asked Fa. 'Just because it's our first run, mind. We can't afford it every trip, and there'll be a good few more of those before we're done here.'

The coffee was lukewarm and weak, but sweet and delicious all the same. Ida and Fa held the liquid in their mouths for a while to make it last, before swallowing slowly. Then Ida put her warmed mittens to her cheeks to use every bit of the warmth they had paid for.

They resumed climbing. Step, step, step, hour after hour. Ida's eyes hurt now, scrunched tight against brightness reflected from the snow. You could get snow blindness, she knew. She'd seen people with it, having to be led by others.

'Hold up!' came a shout from up ahead. Ida braced herself on the slope and eased herself more upright. Her feet were numb and clumsy, yet when she kicked them into the snow they were still able to feel hurt. Fa stood, bent over, in front of her. A long black shadow-silhouette of Fa leaned up the snowy slope beside him, a strange, tall angular creature with a hump on its back and a lump on its front. Everyone in the line had a warped shadow version of themselves thrown off to one side. Grotesque.

Ida kicked her feet. She couldn't feel them at all now. It was as if she had stumps for legs. She thought of the man who had told her in camp how he was 'a few toes short' after getting frostbite. Another man was without an ear for the same reason. His cheeks were burned quite black. Ida tried hard to wriggle her toes within her boots to get the blood flowing back in them.

'How are you doing, my love?' Fa turned to her.

Ida just grunted a sound. Talking seemed too much effort. But Fa lifted a gloved hand from the package that he was carrying, and pointed upwards. Ida looked up properly then and saw that the cloud layer was gone. The top of the pass was not nearly as far away as she had supposed. Of course, she thought, there must be sun for there to be shadows and for her eyes to have been so dazzled by sunshine reflected from the snow. She looked down and felt dizzy at the drop below her, with Sheep Camp satisfyingly tiny and far away. She grinned at Fa properly behind her scarf wrapping and his eyes smiled back.

The line started moving once more, jerk-jerk upwards. But now Ida looked about her as they stamped over the top of the climb in the last low sunshine to see seven great glaciers, glistening strange greeney-blue colours among the snowy peaks of the mountains that still towered all around them.

'Would you ever believe such a thing possible?' she said, quoting a Tilly phrase.

Fa laughed. Then he held a hand to his mouth because the cold had chapped his lips so that they split and hurt when he laughed. There was something else that made Ida laugh – a tatty Union Jack flag waving from a post.

The British flag hung outside the shack office of the Canadian North-West Mounted Police. Bear-like in their great buffalo coats with brass buttons, the Canadian police were checking all who arrived, ensuring that they stacked their goods correctly, that they had the correct forms, and that they paid the correct tax.

'Good evening, young lady!' said one policeman to Ida.

'You're British!' said Ida in surprise.

'Most of us are,' said the young man.

Fa handed over his papers. 'Did many get over the pass early enough to beat the freeze?' he asked. 'Might some have got to Dawson already?'

'A few will have got there,' said the young man, stamping the papers with an official stamp. 'But only those who travelled light, before we brought in the rule that you must take supplies to last through the winter.'

'So they have the advantage of us!' said Fa, hands beginning to dance in indignation. 'Weeks – no, months – ahead of us!'

'Well, yes and no, Mr Metcalf,' said the young man. 'I suspect that those men must be suffering now without supplies. There's little to be bought in Dawson, however much money or gold you have to spend. Millionaires and paupers, they are all in for a hungry time, and the ground and streams are unworkable until the thaw comes.'

'I see,' said Fa. 'Poor chaps.'

Their two porters had started a pile of Metcalf goods, labelling it with a named post, and they had already set off back down the mountain. Fa thumped down his crate and the bundle that he'd carried, adding them to the pile. Ida added her pack and felt wonderfully light without the load dragging at her.

Going down that steep slope was far easier than the upwards trudge had been. They followed the crowd down a longer but less steep route that shone with polished snow because most people sat and slid their way down. The fastest technique seemed to be to sit on your shovel, but many came off and took a tumble, at speed, that way.

'Tuck your coat under you and let's go tobogganing!' said Fa. Whooping dragon breath into the rapidly darkening air, Fa and Ida slid down the mountain in minutes.

'Did you see?' panted Ida at the bottom of the slope, standing up and knocking snow from her coat and rubbing her bruised behind.

'That unfortunate man?' said Fa.

'They'd splinted his leg, so it must have been broken,'

said Ida. The sight and sound of the distressed young man, slung in a tent canvas stretcher and being carried jerkily back down the mountain, had shocked her.

'Poor fellow,' said Fa. 'I imagine that's the end of his prospecting dreams.' What would happen if Fa broke a leg, or I did, wondered Ida?

'We must make sure to look after each other,' said Fa. He's frightened too, thought Ida.

Back in the tent, Ida eased off her boots and stockings and rubbed and rubbed at her stinging and blistered feet.

'I'll mix salt water for you to soak them,' said Fa. 'Rub them in snow first, then into cold water before we warm them properly. That's the only way to avoid frostbite damage.' He peered at a blackening toenail on Ida's foot. 'Not good. I think that we must bind rags over your boots as I've seen others do. Those silly boots of yours aren't up to snowy mountain conditions. Whatever was that salesman thinking of, saying they were just the thing?'

'And we need to stop our faces from becoming burned, or going blind from snow glare,' said Ida. 'Your face is as red as anything.' She laughed and pointed. 'Except there are white lines outwards from your eyes like cat's whiskers where you've scrunched your face tight. Did you see that some people had soot on their faces to keep the sun off? We could do that.'

'Some have sunglasses,' said Fa. 'This is where we begin to discover that we didn't buy all the right things after all.'

'I could make something for our eyes,' said Ida. 'Perhaps some sort of veil.'

'Veils were another thing we didn't think to bring,' laughed Fa.

'But we did!' said Ida. 'We have yards and yards of mosquito netting. We can use some of that in the same way that Minnie's dad used netting with a hat when he went to open his beehives.'

'Well, that is an idea,' agreed Fa.

They were glad of the prepared beans, easy to heat and eat with hunks of stale bread. They ate in silence, each thinking their own thoughts.

Then Fa said, 'Ida, I think that we must let our porters go. We have already spent a great deal of our money and we must be sure to keep enough for travelling home.'

'But we will find gold, won't we?'

'Indeed,' said Fa. 'But you know what Mama always said. "Live in the hope of good luck, but always be prepared for bad. That way it can't catch you out." Besides, there is a very long wait until the spring thaw, so there is plenty of time for carrying all our goods up there ourselves. The exercise will keep us warm and occupied.'

Ida thought of those two tons of goods to be shifted. She thought of the steep agony of the Chilkoot Pass, and of how the weather would get colder, and the days shorter. It was hard not to cry.

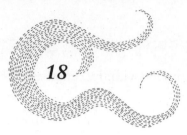

18

Day after day Fa and Ida walked that climb, carrying their goods. Now Ida climbed and walked with a pair of Fa's thick woollen socks over her thin boots, and over that strips of bean sacking, wound and bound and tied tight. It made walking clumsy, but it kept her feet from freezing and it gave better grip than the smooth leather soles.

Ida got sick of her long woollen skirts, gathering snow around the hem and tangling cold and wet and heavy around her legs as she walked, so she borrowed a pair of Fa's breeches and another pair of thick socks to wear inside the boots.

'Just for the climb,' she told Fa. 'Then I'll dress as a girl again.'

'You look like a scarecrow with that string holding the breeches up!' said Fa.

Snow kept falling, the temperature kept dropping, the days kept shortening. Ida and Fa wore veils of mosquito netting to shield their faces and eyes from the glare when the sun shone. If they forgot to protect their eyes, they soon saw the world as a terrifying kind of red-jelly place, quivering. They wrapped scarves all around their faces, leaving only a slit for eyes to peep through, when snow was falling. They walked the 'Chilkoot Lock-Step', an odd, jerky, heaving step upwards, in line with the thousands of others, day after day after day. The thump of feet and groan of the climbers was joined on many days by the moan of an incessant wind that chaffed skin and chilled through however many layers of clothing they bundled themselves in.

Some of their fellow climbers got injured or ill and had to give up the struggle, returning to Dyea, their goods scattered about the mountain. Ida saw men cry. At least one man went mad and shot himself dead. But there were also rare moments of beauty when they saw the Northern Lights, a range of blue-greens and pinks dancing over the silhouetted black shapes of mountains. The way that the colours moved and shimmered reminded Ida of Mama's silk skirts, glinting greens and pinks and mauves. Those colours writhed against a deeply dark sky jewelled with a big glowing moon and bright stars. All that's missing from the sky treasure trove is gold. If you added that, you could make jewellery from the skies, thought Ida. I must remember this and somehow try to describe it all in a letter to Grandmama.

'Fa, could you paint this when we get back to England?'

'I will certainly try,' he said. 'Perhaps, between us, we will remember quite how strange this is. I'm not at all sure that I will believe my memories once we are home unless I have you to compare and confirm them with.'

Through two months of twilight they trudged, sweating and freezing alternately, red-eyed and filthy, hungry and so cold their bones ached as they worked back and forth, up and down. Too cold and tired and cramped to change their clothes, Fa and Ida both smelled bad. On Saturday nights they melted snow and washed themselves a little, but very quickly.

'Mama would not have enjoyed this,' said Fa.

'Do you?' asked Ida.

Fa paused. 'We did say that we wanted an adventure.'

'But I didn't think it would be quite like this,' said Ida.

'I doubt that anybody here did,' said Fa.

There was rest on Sundays, of course, but rest too when blizzards came, making the steep slope impassable for days on end. Then the wind really howled, whipping stinging snow to billow and bury their tent in dark stillness. When that happened, Ida and Fa huddled in blankets and ate cold food and used a bucket for a lavatory. Thank goodness the cold freezes what is in the bucket so that it doesn't smell, thought Ida. But everything else froze too. Any damp clothes were soon as stiff as board. Ida had terrors that her own blood would slow and freeze, making a statue of her. She worked hard at wriggling toes and fingers to keep her blood moving, worrying each time she felt herself slipping into sleep.

'Oh, I'm so bored!' said Ida, as one blizzard went into a third day. 'How do bears stand being in their caves all winter long?'

'They grin and bear it – perhaps that's why they're called

bears!' said Fa. 'Actually I think that they just sleep, don't they? They probably wake up and think that five minutes passed when in fact they've snored through several months of winter.'

'I wish that I could do that!' said Ida, hugging blankets tight around herself and rocking and rocking to get some slight movement into her stiff cold body. 'How much longer will winter go on? What is the date now, Fa? What day is it?'

'It is Friday twenty-fourth December 1897.'

'Christmas Eve!' Ida sat up straight. 'So tomorrow is . . .'

'Christmas Day. An extra day of rest, even if the weather clears. We will think about the birth of Jesus Christ, and we will think about those we have left at home in England.'

'But we d–'

'Actually, I do have a little something for you to look forward to opening.' Fa smiled.

'But I have nothing for you!' said Ida. And no way of buying or making or finding anything either. Ida went very quiet and thought hard as the blizzard moaned moodily outside. She turned her back on Fa and worked open the stiff, frozen canvas sack that held her fountain pen buried deep from the cold within a bundle of clothes. She warmed the pen next to her skin and tore the plain endpaper from the Chicago Record book. Then she began drawing, and crossing out and crumpling up and starting again, until she had a picture of the church in their Norfolk village with the fields and the sea and the houses around it at the top of the page. Under the picture she wrote:

The Bell

I would know where I was in time and space
When I heard the bell
Telling the hour over the marshes from her tower.
Even though I never saw her, swinging and sounding, pealing merrily,
Tolling steadily inside her tower, I heard her and I knew that she was there.
I miss that sound so badly now that I am away from her and her from me.
But if I am still, I can hear my bell telling me steadily how things are and how I should be.
That bell's name is Isabella, my Mama.
And what she's telling me now,
Is to bid merry Christmas to my lovely Fa!

Ida gave that paper to Fa next morning and his reddened eyes cried large weepy tears, but they were accompanied by a smile and a hug.

'Thank you, my love. Thank you.' He closed his eyes for a moment. 'She truly is with us here, I think.' Then Fa handed Ida a small package wrapped in newspaper. 'You will see that we were both thinking in much the same way.'

Ida gently opened up the paper to reveal . . .

'Oh!'

'Yes. It's the brooch that I dared to buy your Mama as the very first token of my affection for her, back when I was a young student in Cambridge, and her brother's friend. It isn't of any great monetary value. I couldn't afford to buy the kind of thing that she was used to at home, of course. But she kept it always.'

'And wore it always,' said Ida, fingering the white portrait of an elegant lady's head, sitting in relief on a blue porcelain background. 'Thank you, Fa.' She pinned the brooch to her inner blouse so that she could feel it safe against her chest and know that it would keep soft and warm and safe there.

Most of the mass of people stopped work for Christmas Day, although just a few couldn't resist the pull of the gold and the chance to get one day ahead of their fellow argonauts. Those men climbed and carried in ones and twos, scattered dots on the slope where there was usually a stream of people.

But Fa and Ida joined with people from neighbouring tents to put together a kind of a Christmas feast. Ida found a bag of almonds and a bag of sugar. She pulled the unused gold panning pan from its pack and put it over the fire, then she tossed in the nuts. They soon began to cook, oozing out their own oil. She poured sugar onto the nuts, to soak into the nut oil. Then she stirred and stirred as the nuts and sugar came stickily together.

'Mmm!' said Fa. 'That smells just about how I imagine Heaven might smell!' Ida took the pan off the fire and set it on the snow to cool.

'Tarnation!' she said, using a word she'd learned in camp. 'It's all gone into one large lump. I wanted separate nuggets like the ones we bought in Seattle. I was going to tie them in pieces of mosquito netting and hang them from that big tree.'

'Let me get my hammer on to it,' said Fa.

So the Metcalfs' presents to their neighbours were bags of sugared nuts to be plucked from a tree that was a little like the one that picture papers liked to show in Queen Victoria's home at Christmas, and which Grandmama had copied at the big house.

Other people brought out delicious baked rabbit stuffed with onions and bread and dried berries, apple pies with spice and dried fruit in them, pancakes with maple syrup, and bottles of beer and whisky. One woman played twangy Christmas carols on a banjo and Ida sang along to the ones she knew. A couple of men did a clog dance in the snow, then they tried to teach the dance to the whole crowd.

'It may not be pretty, but it certainly warms a fellow!' panted Fa.

'You look like one of cousin Eric's string puppets!' laughed Ida, as Fa's arms and legs flailed about.

In the dusky darkness, the group of prospectors sat on logs around a big fire built from wood especially hauled and saved for this day. They drank tea and ate the nut candy and told stories.

Then somebody looked at Ida and asked, 'Tell us what made you come all this way, English girl.'

Ida was embarrassed as all the heads turned their gaze towards her. What should she say? That she was looking for gold would be the obvious answer. But not quite the truth, she thought, and she was in a mood to be truthful with these generous people from all over the world who had gathered to share the day.

'I just, well, I suppose that I wanted to be with my father. To do what he was doing and be together. That's all.'

'Then you're a lucky man, Mr Metcalf,' said somebody. And Ida turned to see Fa's fire-reddened face smile a particularly big smile.

'I most certainly am,' he said, and he reached out an arm to hug Ida around the shoulders.

And that was Christmas enough for Ida; one she would remember forever.

19

The weeks after Christmas were hard. Night never lifted properly into day, only into a gloomy greyness that never showed them the sun. It was a perpetual dusk and it snowed and snowed with howling gales, so they mostly stayed in their tent in Sheep Camp, cold and bored.

Ida saw that Fa was doing what Mama had used to call 'turning in on himself', his face scrunched with thoughts that clearly worried him, but saying nothing.

'Fa,' said Ida, 'What are we going to do with the gold, just supposing that we really do find our own Bonanza Creek kind of a place?'

Fa looked up slowly, then saw from Ida's face that this question was a game. He stretched out his arms and eased his shoulders and neck.

'Weeell,' he said. 'Let me see now. I think that I will buy us a home, before anything else. One with a good fireplace and good gaslights to warm and brighten the winters. And a larder full of such a variety of foods . . . none of it beans and all of it tasty!'

'A home back in Norfolk?'

'Is that what you would like?'

Ida nodded.

'Norfolk it is, then. But a big fine house, with one more floor and one more turret and one more courtyard than your Uncle Stephen and his family have at the big house now. With carriages and stables. Maybe a glasshouse growing peaches and . . .'

But Ida was shaking her head. 'Oh no,' she said. 'I don't want that size or kind of a house, or that life. It would make me too grand above my friends if we lived in a place like that. Besides, we'd need all sorts of servants and you would be hopeless at telling them what to do.'

'True,' said Fa, tugging at his straggly beard. 'Well then, you tell me what you would like to spend the money on. Dresses and jewels?'

'I just want to buy our old cottage by the sea,' said Ida.

'Leaks and mouldy damp walls and all?'

'Yes, but we could afford to have it repaired. Mr Jarvis, Annie Jarvis from school's dad, could help in the garden. We could build a studio for you to paint in. Get a boat, maybe! Oh, and books and things. Nice food. A fire, as you said. Perhaps a kitten. Then, that's about all, I think.'

'Don't you want to show Grandmama that we can do as well as her?' said Fa.

'You mean be as rich as her? Not really. Grandmama has to be grand all the time, even in her own house, because the servants are watching and noticing. I shouldn't like that. But we could buy Grandmama a fine big jewel as a present if you want to show off!'

'That is exactly what we will do, then,' laughed Fa. 'A great big glistening jewel, of a kind that's never been found before, and is worth more than anything that even Queen Victoria owns!' Fa pretended to pin a jewel to his skinny chest as if he was Grandmama, whose chest was a very different shape from his, and Ida laughed.

'Oh, I want to start digging for gold now!' said Fa, rubbing his hands together.

The carrying of heavy clumsy packs up the Chilkoot Pass went on whenever the weather allowed them to escape their tent. One night a team of men cut steps for the top part of the climb, and that made it a little easier. Others added a rope banister that you could pull yourself up along. It was hot work, doing that climb, but you froze so quickly when you stopped – froze to your very core. And the carrying and climbing was never enough, never finished.

We are slaves to a master called Gold, thought Ida. She tried to think again of the good things that gold would bring as reward for all this struggle. It was the only way to make any sense of what they were doing. Or she escaped into daydream. Ida's favourite daydream was to imagine herself lying in a bath-sized steak and mushroom pie, with warm gravy to sink into, soft lumps of meat and vegetables all around her, delicious smelling steam rising hotly up to her face, and a blanket of pastry pulled up to her chin.

It was early in March that Ida and Fa finally cleared

the last of their pile of goods from Sheep Camp. They broke camp and carried the tent and cooking equipment up the Pass, reaching the top just as the moodily boiling snowclouds cleared for a magical few moments of clarity.

'Look, Fa!' said Ida, pointing. Three thousand five hundred feet below them was Dyea, a tiny grubby mess of a town. Ida held up her thumb to blot the whole town from her view.

'No more Dyea and no more Sheep Camp,' said Fa, and he took Ida's shoulders and twisted her around. 'Look over there instead.' Fa nodded towards where Lake Lindeman could be seen glinting silverly, one thousand two hundred feet below them, on the other side of the mountains. Then the clouds closed the view down once more and it was soon hard to see more than three or four yards in any direction.

'Downhill all the way now,' said Fa, and that was a nice thought.

They camped on the summit amongst the ghostly mounds of goods buried under tens of feet of snow. Everything had to be dug out before it could be carried down, but the first trip was to take their tent and bedding and stove, to make themselves a new base by the lakes.

The sun was beginning to show itself again – just a shy blink of light over the horizon, quickly snatched back. But Ida knew that the light would stay longer every day now, growing to proper daylight and warmth. That promise lifted her spirits. Fa's mood was happier too.

It was steep down from the summit of the Chilkoot to frozen Crater Lake, past the stair-step series of lakes Morrow, Long and Deep, before a ten-mile trek to Lake Lindeman. There, to their dismay, they found thousands of tents already set up and settled along the lake rim, and boat making already underway.

'Let's go further on,' said Ida, feeling sudden panic. 'Let's get ahead of all these people.'

'On to Lake Bennett, then,' said Fa. 'Another seven miles.'

Ida had in her mind the idea that they could set-up their tent at the very front of the queue, but when they came to frozen Lake Bennett it was as thickly rimmed with tents as Lake Lindeman had been. Here the Chilkoot Trail from Dyea and the White Pass Trail from Skagway met, so the crowd pushing forward was instantly doubled. Ida eyed those coming from the White Pass warily. They were somehow a different tribe, bonded through different experiences from the Chilkoot Pass agonies that she had shared with the familiar faces on their path. But it was interesting to hear tales from those who had taken that alternative route.

'Dead horses, that's what it was like. Just dead horses and more dead horses. You walked on dead horses,' one gaunt boy told her. I'd rather climb ice steps than walk on dead horses, thought Ida. But there would be no horses or walking for the next part of the journey. Now they must turn their minds to making the fastest kind of a boat they possibly could. Ida looked around at tens of thousands of other people thinking those same things. Fa and I know nothing about making boats, she thought.

20

The tents around Lake Bennett were of all sorts. Tent hotels, tent barbers, tent saloons, tent casinos, tent chapels, tents for fortune tellers, as well as thousands upon thousands of tent homes. Alongside the tents were mountains of supplies, crates and furniture, stoves, tins, sacks, suitcases, sleds, boots, a few skinny tethered horses and goats, and all sorts of everything else, all being added to by the second as teams trudged into camp with packs of goods brought down the mountains. The air was full of sawdust and the smell of freshly butchered pine, loud with noises of sawing and swearing and hammering. The lakeside was cluttered with piles of logs and cut timber and part-made, crude sorts of boats.

Ida and Fa hurried to find a pitch for their own tent. 'We can have a proper fire with wood for free,' said Ida. 'I'll fetch some.'

Between the tents and the woods was a huge area of tree stumps where trees had been felled for boat making and fuel for fires. A cry of 'Timber!' went up every so often as another tree came crashing down, to be lugged and sawed and stacked and cut to size. Ida gathered an armful of twigs and branches that lay around the fallen timbers, then she headed back to the lakeside camp, beginning to panic when she realised that their base had already been swallowed up by more newcomers and she couldn't instantly find it.

'Ah, there you are,' said Fa as she threw down her scratchy bundle. 'Just look what I've got!' Fa pointed.

'A sledge?' said Ida.

'A sledge,' said Fa. 'I traded it with a man who had lost his bag of nails down a crevasse and was desperate for some in order to complete his boat. He has no further use for the sledge, so an exchange was ideal.'

'But don't we . . .'

'Need all our nails ourselves?' said Fa. 'We had more than enough. The important thing is that the sledge will speed up our trips to bring all our goods down, so it will allow us to begin boatbuilding sooner than otherwise.' Fa patted the sledge as if it was a pack pony that he was fond of. 'See that?' Fa pointed to a canvas bundle. 'She even has a sail to help move her along.'

The sledge did make it much easier to haul the goods they dug from the snow at the top of the mountain the next day. The sledge, piled high, took far more than the two of them could carry in a trip. And it was so easy! Going downhill, they had to do little more than steer the sledge and help it over and around the bumps.

It was especially good over the iced-over lakes. 'Just don't melt quite yet, please,' Ida told the lake, as she pushed and Fa pulled. Once out on the lake ice, they erected the square sail and set it at an angle to pick up the breeze. The sledge took off on its own, with Fa and Ida stumbling and laughing after it.

'It's alive!' shouted Ida. She threw herself over the packed sledge and let herself be wonderfully swooped over the ice.

The days slowly lengthened as Fa and Ida worked back and forth, back and forth, sledging their goods down to the lake. Even with the sledge, it took day after day to reduce the pile at one end and build it again at the other. At the top of the Pass, people were still pouring upwards from Dyea and Skagway. The glaciers shone turquoise and sapphire on dull days, dazzling white when the sun shone through, mauve and pink and green at twilight when the going was slow and they were travelling back late. As the days warmed and lengthened, the camps around the lakes grew and grew. More trees were felled and made into planks, and those planks became boats. But Fa and Ida still hadn't begun to make a boat. Fa tugged at his beard. It had grown so long and straggly it now rested on his chest.

'I'm not shaving this beard until we have hauled the very last pack to the lake,' he said.

'You might be tripping over your beard by then,' said Ida.

Blizzards still shut Fa and Ida in their tent for occasional days on end, but the world was warming and the days becoming brighter for longer.

'The snow is getting softer,' said Fa. 'And so is the ice.'

The lakes began to creak ominously under the weight of people and goods and sledges. There were occasional rolling rumbles from the mountain tops where avalanches of softened snow, piled high and heavy, let go of their perches and sluiced down the mountain sides.

'It's getting more dangerous by the day,' said Fa. 'The sooner we've finished with that mountain the happier I will be.' They packed the sledge with the very last crates from their mountain-top pile on April Fool's Day.

'How appropriate, since here we are chasing a darn-foolish dream, in the company of thousands of like-minded fools,' laughed Fa. 'Still, we're done with this particular foolishness. Time now for us fools to build a boat.'

But the season of Chilkoot Pass foolishness was not yet over for everyone. Three days later news came into camp of a terrible avalanche.

'Dozens killed,' said one man, shaking his head. 'Not one Indian was on the mountain, because they knew the dangers in the conditions. They told people. The Mounties, too, warned folks. Lord, anyone with an ounce of sense could see the danger of the soft snow, but greed or madness got the better of them to such a degree that they couldn't abide to let just one more day go by between them and their gold. It surely makes you think.'

Sixty-five lives lost, they said. Sixty-five families who wouldn't know for weeks to come that their father or brother or son was dead.

Because they were done with the Chilkoot, Fa shaved his beard to reveal a pale chin that contrasted with the top of his face. But any feeling of celebration had died along with those prospectors on the Pass.

Before Mama got ill, Ida and Fa had sometimes been out on Jim's fishing boat off the Norfolk coast, but Ida didn't think that Fa knew anything more about boats than how to sit in one and perhaps pull on a rope if he was told to. Now Fa brought out paper and a pencil and drew boats. They were lovely pictures, but they weren't practical plans.

'Why do you put in waves and birds and things?' asked Ida. 'You need diagrams with measurements and joints and things, don't you?'

'I need to picture a boat in action before I can think of those details,' said Fa. But Ida suspected that he was putting off something he didn't feel confident about. So she went looking and listening around the boats being built by their neighbours to see if she could learn any lessons. She thought of the instructions that God gave to Noah; exact measurements for building his ark. That's what they needed now. Clear plans and the wood with which to carry out those plans.

Walking along the lakeside littered with boat builders, it was clear that there was no single idea about the shape of boat best suited for the job ahead. There were square-ended boats, round-ended boats and sharp-ended triangular boats. Some were big: huge square rafts with walls around their edges. Some were even big enough to carry horses or cattle and quite a group of people. Others were so small that they were no more than three or four logs strapped together to carry just a single man and a few bags. Some had sails, some paddles or poles, or a combination of those things. There were canoes too, either the collapsible canvas kind that people had bought and then hiked over the mountains, or logs from the woods, laboriously hollowed-out. Indians were selling light canoes made out of animal hides. Those looked strong and fast. But how would the people in canoes carry all their goods? Part of the answer to that question was clear.

'Flour for sale!' called a skinny young man. 'Do you want a good warm blanket, Miss? Or a tin of molasses? All at very reasonable prices.' He had a rough table set out with things he wanted to sell. Of course, the law didn't require him to have the full ton of goods now that he was over the Canadian border. But won't he need the stuff once he gets to the Klondike, wondered Ida? Is it best to get there fast and find the gold, or best to be able to survive even if we don't find gold?

You could learn a lot just wandering around, watching and listening:

'Reckon we should grease the bottom – make it slip slick through the water.'

'Dog'll have to go. Too darn heavy, and liable to move about and upset the craft.'

Ida heard quarrels too. There were two men at a saw frame, one above and one under the log, working a long two-handled saw.

'Hiram, you doing anything down there? Seems to me I've got all the work lifting and cutting, while you just hang on that saw and let your weight pull the dang thing down! Why, you ain't even doing that! I'm having to push down as well as pull up!'

A furious, coughing, spitting Hiram shouted back, 'Well, if it's so darn easy down in the pit, why don't you try it for size yourself, Jez? I'd sooner be above the sawdust anytime!'

Ida watched as the two red-faced men in shirtsleeves threw looks of loathing at one another and swapped places. And it wasn't long before, 'Are you attempting to make me lose my temper? 'Cos if you are, you're doing a darn fine job of it! Pull, man, pull!' And they were off again as the big saw juddered and stuck and hardly moved an inch. Ida laughed.

'Most of these fellas never done a day's labouring in their lives afore they came out here. No idea at all how to carry on,' said an elderly man sitting on the side of a boat. His looked like a proper well-built boat. It didn't have the crude rough chunkiness that most of the others had.

'Is your boat finished?' asked Ida.

The man nodded. 'Done this trip a few times afore, so I've got myself familiar with the job, and that always makes a thing go faster.'

'What sort of boat would be the best kind to make for two people, do you think?' asked Ida. 'Two people who don't know much about making boats or sailing.'

'Well, now,' the old man stroked his chin. 'I'd aim for a rowboat, with a mast and sail as well, and a pole for pushing and steering. You'll meet all kinds of waters on the Yukon and they each of them need handling differently. Make the boat flat-bottomed and wide, so's you can store your goods secure and even-loaded. Strap it all down so it don't shift none and tip you over.' Then he looked Ida up and down. 'Why, are you thinking of building such a boat yourself, young lady?'

'My father and I are,' said Ida. 'Thank you for your advice.'

'Oh, you're more than welcome, Miss. You just come along here any time and ask some more when you hit a snag,' he said. 'All I'm doing is sitting here and waiting for that ice to melt, so I may as well be useful to others.'

But when Ida got back to the tent, she found that Fa had plans of his own. He waved an arm in an extravagant circle. 'I've had the most marvellous piece of luck this afternoon, Ida. I met an Englishman – one of just the right sort – and he's keen as anything to join forces with us.'

'To make a boat together?'

'That's it.'

'But what do you mean, he's "the right sort"?' asked Ida. 'Does he know about boats?'

'All about them!' grinned Fa. 'Tells me that he rowed at Cambridge. Not my college, but much the same time as me, as it turns out. Knows your Uncle Stephen. Rowed with him, and was even in the same regiment for a couple of years. Isn't that a piece of luck?'

'But that kind of rowing boat is different from the ones they're making here, isn't it?' Ida had seen a photograph of Uncle Stephen and some other men standing stiffly, arms folded, all with big moustaches, in front of a long skinny rowing boat called an eight. 'That's not the sort of boat to carry boxes and stuff on. There are rocks and rapids in the water. Wouldn't a boat like that tip over?'

'Well, maybe,' admitted Fa, his arms coming down. 'But a boat is a boat and you can just tell by talking to this chap that he knows about water and boating and such.' Fa chuckled. 'His name is Mr Selwyn Stanley. He's on his own now. His brother couldn't cope with the Pass and turned for home. But Stanley carried on, using porters. He's got money, it seems, but no company. Tells me that he has eaten nothing but beans, rice and rancid bacon for weeks and longs for a change of diet. Could you rustle up one of your dried apple pies? I've invited him over. You'll see for yourself what a splendid fellow he is.'

It was nice to see Fa enthusiastic, so Ida made an apple

pie. It was one of the many skills she'd picked up in the camps. She put dried apple and raisins to soak in water. Then she made a hard, tough kind of pastry from flour and water and a small amount of precious canned butter. She lined a baking tin with the grey pastry, then put in her apple filling, over which she carefully spooned sugar and some of the ground cinnamon they had brought with them, before flopping the pastry lid on top. She slit the pastry to let steam out, then made a little boat from the left-over pastry dough and secured that to the pie lid, so as to use every last scrap of food and to give good luck to the boat meeting tonight. She made the pastry boat as near to the shape of the boat the old man had made, hoping to give Fa and his new friend a hint. Then she put the pie into their small stove oven and prepared the rest of the meal for their guest.

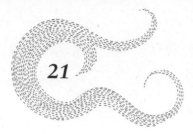

21

Mr Stanley greeted Ida by doffing his hat and making a little bow, as if she were a proper lady. He was younger than Fa, which seemed strange when they had been at university at the same time. Mr Stanley must be very clever and have gone there early, Ida decided. He had a big moustache, and when he sat beside the fire a smell came off him that suggested he didn't wash as often as he might. Perhaps that is what happened when you travelled alone? Ida shuffled to sit a little further away from him.

They ate the meal, but Ida was reluctant to clear the dishes and wash them for fear of missing out on interesting conversation. So she took a rounded pebble she had collected earlier from the lakeside and slipped it inside one of Fa's socks that had worn through. She sat and darned the sock over the pebble, as she had seen Tilly darn over a wooden mushroom back at the big house, weaving the wool, criss-cross, tightly together to build up a patch.

And she listened to the men's talk of timber and saw mills, pegs and nails, sails and paddles and prices. They talked of staking a claim and mining for gold together once the boat arrived in the Klondike area. Ida felt that they were getting what Mama would call 'a little ahead of themselves'. A boat was surely all they needed to think about just now.

'How long will it take to build a boat?' asked Ida, and the two men looked up.

'Gosh, useful daughter you have there, Metcalf!' said Mr Stanley, noticing Ida's darning work. 'I say, you could do the same for my socks, Miss Metcalf. That is, if your father and I are to be partners.'

Fa's eyes twinkled at Ida's indignant scowl. 'Stanley has a plan for a boat, Ida. He's willing to pool his resources with us. We will build a boat together, travel together, and then work together to find gold. That means we shan't need to duplicate everything. We can leave some of this stuff behind and lighten our load. Isn't that marvellous?'

Ida supposed that it was, although she felt a little sick at the thought of abandoning things they had struggled so hard to bring this far.

'Speed is everything!' said Mr Stanley.

'It certainly is,' said Fa.

Mr Stanley produced a hip flask and took a swig from it. 'Care for some, Metcalf?'

'Well, why not? To celebrate a new partnership, eh?' said Fa.

'What shape of prow will the boat have?' said Ida.

'Goodness, she's a girl who cares about the technicalities of building boats! My sisters would never have had the slightest interest in such a thing,' said Mr Stanley.

'Perhaps your sisters don't put themselves and all their belongings into boats to be made by people who have little idea how to build a boat,' countered Ida. There was something about Mr Stanley that annoyed her intensely.

'Now then, Ida,' said Fa, frowning. But he did say to Mr Stanley, 'The shape is important, of course. Have you any thoughts?'

'Narrow and V-shaped to slip through the water fast,' said Mr Stanley, chopping the air with his hands to demonstrate.

'But how could we stack flat crates within a V-shape?' asked Ida, winding her wool and standing up.

Mr Stanley took a long suck on his pipe, then blew the smoke in Ida's direction before turning to Fa. 'I must say, I didn't think it was considered ladylike to be quite so sharp as your daughter appears to be, Metcalf.'

'Ida, the dishes,' said Fa quietly. There was a kind of apology in his eyes. Ida slammed the tin plates together as the men took another swig from Mr Stanley's hip-flask. Whatever was in that flask had the same smell as Mr Stanley.

'A game of cards, Metcalf? Let's make a gentlemanly evening of it.'

Ida found that one of the thousands of tents in the camp had a painted wooden sign declaring it to be a post office. So she wrote again to Grandmama.

Beside Lake Bennett

8 May 1898

Dear Grandmama,

I do hope that you are exceedingly well because we are.

I write this sitting on a log in sunshine. We still have snow over almost everything, but it is now melting into mud, especially around the tents. There are purple flowers with hairy stems coming up, despite the snow. My neighbour, Mrs Travis, tells me that these flowers are called pasque flowers, meaning something to do with Easter. There are blue harebells in the woods too, and something pink and pretty which I cannot name. Water is running under the moss and stones. I can hear it. Yet the dirty old ice on the lakes still holds.

You will be amused to learn that Fa and I spend all our work days at present building a boat. Fa is working with an Englishman called Mr Selwyn Stanley. Mr Stanley once rowed a Cambridge eight in the races they call bumps, and he knows Uncle Stephen. Is that not a coincidence? You see how we are in quite respectable company! Mr Stanley thinks himself something of an expert on boats. But he and Fa could not agree on quite what shape of boat to build, so it is lucky we have the help of an elderly American gentleman called Ted.

You will think me impertinent to call him that, but he says that he has no surname. Fa thinks that Ted chooses to have no surname because he is on the run from the law, or more likely on the run from a wife and family he no longer wants. But Ted is such a steady man, and so kind with advice and with turning his hand to helping to make our boat, that I cannot believe he is on the run from anything. To tell the truth, I don't think that our boat would be nearly as advanced as it is without Ted's help.

Fa, Mr Stanley and I have all had much to learn about the craft of boatmaking. The last weeks have been spent in the sawing of wood and the banging of nails. Both Fa and Mr Stanley have black thumbnails where they have missed with the hammer. Mr Stanley makes far more fuss over his thumb, getting me to bandage it, whilst Fa simply gets on with things.

Fa spends every hour of the day (and the days are long now) working on the boat. The trees he cuts down with the axe are still frozen to the core, so very hard to chop. Fa makes a great 'Huh!' noise every time the axe hits, and I know that it hurts his arms because it bounces back so fiercely, having made only a small dent in the tree. You may be glad to know that Fa refuses to let me try my hand with the *axe, but I have done much of the work in making the oars. Fa cut a rough oar shape from a plank, then I used a drawknife to shape it in the way that Ted taught me. I am quite proud of the two oars I have made.*

Mr Stanley is often visiting others in the camp as he researches quite how the boatbuilding should go, so does less work directly on the boat than Fa and I do. Fa says that Mr Stanley knows more about boats, so we must allow him time to think and plan. Fa says that he will 'be worth his weight in gold' once the rowing begins. Mr Stanley found sawing the wood altogether too hard because he has some ailment in his right arm, as well as the sore thumb, so he and Fa were about to pay for others to do the job in a sawpit. Mr Stanley seems to have a great deal of wealth, so doesn't mind the idea of paying for such services, whilst Fa and I are more careful with our spending.

As it turned out, one of the saw men was ill because he had not eaten fresh food for so long. His friends said that his trouble was the scurvy and they had seen other men made blind or even dead of the condition. Then I remembered that an Indian lady had made me buy a packet of native medicine back in Dyea (she swapped it for a button off my coat!). I had no idea what the medicine was for but, when I told the men, they knew of it as an Indian cure and they said it was just what was needed. They brewed some of the dried plants, which they said must be spruce-bark tea, in a kettle of water and made their friend drink it. It took some days, but it seems to have made him better. For that service, they cut wood for Fa at no charge, so I was glad that the medicine proved useful.

I work on the boat itself, as well as on the oars. I hand the men things such as nails when they ask and I am also smoothing the wood in places by scraping it with a piece of broken glass. We don't want splinters where we will sit. I am also stitching a sail from the canvas we bought joined to the sail from our sledge, and even some of Fa's large handkerchiefs. So, you may tell Tilly that my needlework is advancing into the art of patchwork these days.

I have also done most of the caulking and pitching of the boat where the wooden planks join. That is an important, but messy, job because the boat will leak if it is not done thoroughly and well. We tend to work with our neighbouring camp members with such jobs, all turning to work on one boat at a time, but getting each boat finished faster as a result. It is strange to think that we are in a kind of race with all these people who have become our friends.

I do most of the cooking, preparing big meals for

Fa and Mr Stanley because they get so very hungry (as do I) with all the work. But sometimes the cooking is shared amongst neighbours too, so many evenings become quite jolly occasions as a dozen or so people all share a meal around one large fire. Out here we wash the dishes by rubbing them with clean snow (although there is hardly any clean snow to be found now), or we use river sand to scour the pans. So, you can see that life is busy, even though we have remained in the same place for some weeks now.

Fa says that the boat should be complete and ready to load within the next few days. Ted has inspected it and declared it 'riverworthy', and I trust his judgement. It is not a pretty boat, being too square and solid for that, but I have grown fond of her because we have worked so hard to make her. I think she will look after us in return for our labours. So now we wait for the ice to thaw from the lakes and river. Already the ice makes groaning and cracking sounds that Fa says show that water is moving under it. This letter will speed to Dawson by dogsled, but we will not be far behind. And then we shall start our search for gold in earnest.

Can you guess what name we plan to paint on our boat, along with the number we are given? Isabella. I hope that pleases you as it does Fa and me. Mr Stanley may have other ideas in mind, but Fa and

I shall hold out for Isabella whatever his opinion might be on this matter.

Once we reach Dawson I expect I shall be able to write more frequently than I have managed these last months.

Your loving,

Ida

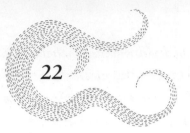

22

One night in May, Ida woke to what sounded like a pistol shot being fired frighteningly close by.

'Fa?' Ida sat up in the dark, her heart thumping high in her throat. Fa sat up too, hair on end, listening intently as a buzz of chatter rose in the tents all around them. Then somebody called out,

'It's the ice! Cracking big time! It's breaking up at last! Yeeee-ha, this is it, folks!'

And suddenly everyone was laughing and cheering from all around.

'So.' Fa clapped his hands together. 'Thank the good Lord that our Isabella is finished and we are ready. I do hope that our friend Stanley has his goods packed and ready to stow.'

The sky lightened very early now, so by 4 a.m. the whole camp was seething with activity. It reminded Ida of when one of the gardeners at the big house had chopped open an anthill and instantly there were ants busy all over, carrying things and working together to rebuild their home. Now it was people carrying goods and stowing them into boats, whilst others desperately sawed and hammered, in danger of being left behind if they couldn't finish their boats quickly.

Mr Stanley did little of their packing, taking an age to take down and bundle his tent. 'I have strained my arm again and it is most painful. Are you not sorry for me, Miss Ida?'

'The arm had no trouble lifting your flask to your lips last night,' said Ida coldly.

'Oh, so sharp – ouch!' said Mr Stanley, and he smiled at her with hard eyes.

'Let us get on with packing this boat, if you please!' said Fa, scowling at the two of them. 'See those canoes already setting forth? This is a race!'

'So it is,' said Mr Stanley. 'A good bit of sport.' More than sport, thought Ida. Our chances of finding a gold-bearing claim depend upon our speed. Is Mr Stanley so very rich already that he doesn't actually care very much about finding gold? Whilst he couldn't carry much, Mr Stanley had opinions aplenty.

'That large crate of mine to go in first, I fancy,' he said. 'My sacks of food packed around it. That's it, Metcalf. Good man. Do make sure that the canvas is well tucked around it all. I shouldn't like my provisions to get damp and spoiled, you know.'

Only once Mr Stanley's pile of goods was all aboard were any of Fa and Ida's added on top.

'That means that the only food accessible on the trip will be our food,' said Ida. 'What will you eat on the way, Mr Stanley?'

'Don't be foolish, Ida,' said Fa. 'We shall all eat from whatever is to hand and then we will equal things up at the other end of the journey.'

'Just so,' said Mr Stanley. 'Er, Metcalf, could you just pay this fellow off for me?' He pointed to the boy who had carried his goods to the boat. 'I realise that I have inadvertently packed my wallet in one of the lower bundles and it would delay us if I were to stop and search it out now. I will of course make up the payment with you once we reach Dawson. Fair's fair, and all that.'

The Canadian police were keeping tally of boats leaving the lakes that day.

'Over eight hundred so far,' they told Fa when he asked.

'Most of them carrying several prospectors each,' said Fa, with a worried frown. 'Step aboard quickly, Ida, and I'll push us off.' Mr Stanley was already comfortably seated.

Ida stood and used the long pole to push away from land as Fa waded in the freezing waters. He shoved their heavily laden boat out into water that was still littered with large chunks of ice. All around, others were launching too and the shouting and cheering thrilled through Ida's body. She was scared of what lay ahead, but also excited; they were on their way to the gold fields at last. Ida sat herself down on a crate as Fa settled to the oars.

'Five hundred miles to go,' she said, as Fa heaved back on the oars, levering them through the mint-green water.

He winked at Ida. 'We'll hoist your sail once we're in open water and then I can sit back and snooze all the way downstream.'

But there was no snoozing for Fa yet. Glancing around at the strange flotilla of craft all around them, he rowed hard, trying to steer clear of others and to pull ahead of the pack. His face was soon red with effort and glistening with sweat, but so were the faces of the hundreds of other rowers around them.

'Stanley?' said Fa, nodding towards the oars.

'Oh, not with my arm as it is, old man,' said Mr Stanley. 'And you're doing splendidly.'

Around them were canoes holding just one man, and scows crammed with poor skinny oxen and horses and dogs. There were rafts made from logs lashed together, and one man simply sat on his sledge with a log strapped either side of it.

'He won't be dry for long!' laughed Fa.

There were junks and skiffs and catamarans, lots and lots of crudely made boats of rectangular or oval or triangular or round shape, with sails and poles and oars, and even mini paddle-steamer paddles.

'Like the Henley Regatta gone mad,' said Mr Stanley.

They left behind the lakeside landscape of mud and tree stumps and sawpits and rubbish, moving into fresh territory. This new landscape had greenery and trees on either side and a view of snow still capping the tops of mountains that seemed to glimmer blue in the sunshine. Then a fresh breeze suddenly breathed over them all, prompting a flurry of excitement and action as people raised sails to catch that free source of power. It was good to get away from the smells of camp and into clean air.

'Hold that, girl,' instructed Stanley, as he tied Ida's triangle of sail to the mast. Ida held the boom. 'Move it over,' said Mr Stanley. 'Move it! Catch that wind or it'll be of no use at all.'

'Ah, this is where Mr Stanley's expertise comes to bear. Do as he says, Ida,' said Fa.

Fa went on rowing, even as the heavy boat slowly increased speed under them. Some boats had sails of proper sail cloth, but many sails were like jolly flags – made from towels and tents and clothes – fluttering in the sunshine.

'Gracious,' said Fa. 'I do believe those ladies have made a sail from their undergarments. Whatever would your Grandmama make of such a display?'

Ida laughed. Her arms soon ached from holding the boom against the tug of the wind. Stanley annoyed her with his barked orders to move this way or that. Fa was working hard and getting tired, and his hands sore. But Ida was happy to be on the move, happy to be on the last leg of their journey, happy to see Fa's excitement bubbling through his exhaustion.

'To think that I should be sitting in a schoolroom and missing this!' said Ida.

'And I at some desk in a bank,' laughed Fa. 'Tell us, Stanley, what occupation have you escaped from to come here?'

'Just some very dull business ventures.'

'Have you a family back in England?' asked Ida.

'No wife or children yet, if that's what you're asking. But noble ancestors galore.' Mr Stanley waved a hand to dismiss the conversation. 'I say, shall I take a turn at the oars, Metcalf? I think that my arm could cope after all.'

So Mr Stanley took the oars and rowed clumsily for a time, letting Fa rest with Ida, enjoying the sunshine and view. It struck Ida that Fa had grown so thin you could see the bones under his skin, whilst Mr Stanley remained well-plumped.

By evening, with the Arctic sun still shining golden light on the mist over the lake, the breeze suddenly dropped and the boats all drifted to a stop, with those rowing and paddling trying to keep going a little longer. Still, a feeling of calm seemed to lull the flotilla into accepting that the race had halted for the night now. Singing came from a few boats, and laughter.

'Mama would have enjoyed this part,' said Ida.

23

As the days passed, the closely packed flotilla began to string out, with the fast, light, sleek-shaped boats at the front and the clumsily built, overpacked boats and rafts at the back. The *Isabella* was keeping pace with some much finer looking boats.

'We're not doing badly,' said Fa. 'A chap just told me they reckon there are more than seven thousand boats on this river now. Extraordinary!'

Fa did most of the rowing, although Mr Stanley did some. He didn't seem very good at it. 'Different kind of boat to handle from our rowing eights at Cambridge,' he said.

Ida tried rowing too. It was very hard work because the boat was clumsy and its weight made it 'like rowing an elephant' according to Fa.

'Chuck some stuff overboard,' suggested Mr Stanley. 'It's ridiculous to be carting quite so much. We won't need it all if we're to work together.'

'Are we going to work together?' said Ida.

There was discussion all day long about what to keep and what to abandon. That evening they lifted ashore Fa and Ida's battered, rusting stove and left it there when they set off again next morning.

'My stove will be quite adequate for the three of us,' said Mr Stanley. Ida quietly mourned the stove she'd learned to coax into warmth, and on which she had cooked their food for months. It felt like abandoning a friend.

After the lakes, the water narrowed into a fast-running river.

'There's a sign!' said Ida. There was a piece of red calico waving a danger warning. It was attached to a wooden board on which was written CANNON.

'The Miles Canyon,' said Fa. 'So, we're about to come to our first rapids. I think that Stanley and I should take an oar each and use them either side, in Indian style, to steer. The water will carry us forward, but we must try and keep to the deep water as much as possible. Ida, perhaps you could have the pole handy in case we come up against any rocks.'

After working so hard to move the heavy boat over the almost still waters of the lake, the current now swept it along at a speed that would cause catastrophe if it were to sweep them into rocks. All three of them braced themselves with oars and a pole as the sides of a gorge rose steeply on either side, cutting out the sunlight and funnelling the river to a foaming torrent.

It wasn't just rocks they had to look out for. There were sandbars to trap them and bits of timber lurching at them from the waves. Those timbers came from boats that had been ahead of them, but were now completely wrecked.

They passed one smashed boat and two men clinging to rocks.

'Can't we help them?' shouted Ida. But she knew that they couldn't because already they were swept beyond the accident and there was no way to get back again.

'We must pray,' said Fa, unexpectedly and firmly. 'Pray for their safety, and for ours too.' He's frightened, Ida realised, and she clutched the heavy pole more tightly. Please, God, keep us safe. Keep everybody safe! And she suddenly thought of stout grand Grandmama, down on her knees in that little church where Mama was buried. She is praying for us, thought Ida. Please make Grandmama as well as she looks.

'Look out!' Ahead of them was a whirlpool, a canoe circling in its waters as the three men in it tried desperately to paddle free from the swirling water's powerful grip.

'Keep to the right!' shouted Mr Stanley. Fa plunged his oar deep into the water on the right side of their boat, holding it down to break the boat's speed on that side and steer it that way, as Stanley paddled from the left. Too far! They were heading towards the steep gorge-side, so Ida scrambled over the packing boxes and thrust her pole to hit the stone and fend them away from it. The boat lurched as she hit, tipping it away from danger, but also crashing Ida so hard onto the pile of crates that two of them were cast overboard. Gone. And the pole in Ida's hands was wrenched away from her as it struck the side. Now the pole was in the water, bucking beside the boat and threatening to spear them.

'I'm sorry!' said Ida. 'I've lost the pole, and . . . oh, sorry!'

But a lost pole and a couple of crates of food was a small price to pay. Other boats tipped over completely and lost all they had.

That was the day that the river trip stopped feeling like any kind of jaunt. After the whirlpool came the Squaw Rapids, tipping and tossing them as they fought with the oars to control the boat that was now leaking where the planks joined.

'I think that your goods at the bottom of the boat must be getting quite damp,' Ida told Mr Stanley.

'Then I fear the caulking and pitching of the boat cannot have been done very well, Miss Metcalf.' Mr Stanley glared at Ida, then smiled his tiger smile. 'We are to divide all fairly between us once we arrive, are we not? In which case the damaged goods will be part of that division.'

'As will the lost goods,' countered Ida.

All this was hissed between them at a volume that Fa wouldn't hear. It was a wet, bedraggled and rather silent Fa, Mr Stanley and Ida who made camp on the riverbank beyond the rapids that night. Once the boat was secured, Mr Stanley threw himself down on a mossy piece of ground and declared:

'Well, I am quite spent.'

Fa, making a tally of the remaining luggage, frowned. Ida pushed her straggly hair behind an ear. 'Please could you find your stove, Mr Stanley,' she said. 'Otherwise I cannot make us a hot meal.'

Ida was so exhausted she could hardly think. Every muscle ached, she was bruised and wet and cold. And mosquitoes buzzed and bit, needing to be slapped away. Fa put a hand on her shoulder. He looked at Mr Stanley and said, 'I propose that Mr Stanley does the cooking tonight.'

Mr Stanley opened his mouth to protest, but Fa gave him a firm look. 'Is there any reason why we shouldn't all take turn and turn about? After all, Ida has worked as hard as either of us today, yet she is a child and we are grown men.'

'Well, I mean to say . . .' began Mr Stanley.

'That's decided, then,' said Fa.

Mr Stanley looked hard at Ida. 'Fetch me the food to be cooked, Miss, and I'll do it.'

Fa made Ida settle into a roll of blanket as soon as the meal was over. She listened to the sound of dishes being washed and packed and a hissed argument of some kind between the two men. She pulled the blanket over her head to cut out the insects and the argument and was soon asleep.

The hundreds of miles of river below the rapids were deep and swift-flowing. The water swelled with the rapidly melting snow pouring down the mountains around the head of the river, flushing the boats down towards the sea. Cliffs either side of gorges glowed yellow in midday sunshine and turned dark purple in evening shadow. Golden eagles swung in the sky overhead and ravens kaarked in the trees. At night wolves howled. The mosquitoes bit their faces to swollen redness, unless they trapped mosquito netting between hat and neck. And all the time there was the splashing and shouting and cursing of other prospectors.

Ida, Fa and Mr Stanley became adept at working their crude boat through the waters, only occasionally juddering to a sickening halt on sandbanks or crashing into rocks or chunks of ice that tore at the timbers and made repairs necessary. There were more rapids. At Five Finger, Mr Stanley leaned out too far, to try and catch an oar that had been dropped by one of the other boats, and he tumbled overboard. Ida's first reaction was to laugh, then she felt bad and tried to look serious before realising that Fa, too, was chuckling and not making any instant move to rescue Mr Stanley. There was no danger of drowning in such water if you could swim, but it was cold.

'Get me out!' shouted Mr Stanley, through chattering teeth. Fa threw him a rope and he and Ida hauled Mr Stanley back on board, where he made a great point of trying to make Fa and Ida almost as wet as he was.

'Take me ashore and make a fire. Feed me brandy!'

demanded Mr Stanley, hand to his forehead like some swooning lady in a theatrical play. Fa and Ida caught each other's eyes and tried not to laugh.

After that, Ida worried that she too might end up in the river at some point, so she took the precious brooch from where it was pinned to her blouse and stowed it. together with the mother of pearl pen. in the canvas bag where Fa kept money and papers, buried deep within the packing.

When the sun shone, Ida felt a kind of happy peace. They didn't row now, simply used the oars to steer away from danger, or into the bank when they needed to camp. The Yukon River itself swept towards the gold, and Ida felt a fondness for the river for that. On its low banks and broad valley bottom were hazy blue patches of bluebells and lupins, amongst the bright green of new grassy growth. There were occasional hares and birds to be seen, and moose and even a black bear coming to the river's edge to drink. Geese flew overhead with creaking wings.

'If only I had a gun!' said Mr Stanley, holding a pretend gun. 'Bang! We'd have feathers for our pillows, foie gras and roast goose to eat, quills to write with . . .'

'There will be berries for picking before long, if the book is to be believed,' said Fa. 'And I dare say there will be other fresh food we can find.'

The thought of food that didn't come from a sack or a tin played in Ida's mind, making her mouth water. When they stopped to camp that night, Ida went searching and found dandelions. Alice from school kept rabbits for selling at market and she fed them dandelion leaves, so they couldn't be poisonous.

Ida made a small salad of dandelion leaves to go with an omelette made from evaporated eggs and chunks of bacon.

'Food fit for gods!' declared Fa.

'Not too bad,' agreed Mr Stanley.

Two boats sailed past them as they sat there and Ida saw Fa wince. 'I really think that we should keep travelling both night and day, now that there hardly is any night. Take the steering in turns, and sleep and eat on board . . .'

'What about . . . ?' began Ida.

Fa waved a hand. 'Well, yes, we will need to set ashore once in a while, for necessary purposes, but not for these indulgent picnics and overnight stops; not while others keep going night and day.'

'Very well,' said Mr Stanley. 'But just now I do have a slight chill.' He sniffed. 'Caused by not being allowed to dry out after my misfortune at the rapids, so I really must sleep and build up my strength once more before I take the helm. I shall sleep for the first shift and then take my turn.'

Stanley needed to drink whisky to help ease his chill and to help him sleep. That seemed to send him so soundly to sleep that it was left to Fa and Ida between them to steer or to sleep, turn and turn about all through that night.

'To tell the truth,' said Fa quietly, 'I'm more at ease with you in charge of the boat than Stanley. You've more sense by far.' That thought glowed warm in Ida as she fought tiredness to steer as well as she possibly could.

Other smaller rivers joined the Yukon, as did more boats of prospectors coming along those tributaries. The biggest of those rivers, entering the Yukon from their right, was the Pelly River. Almost opposite, on the left bank, was the town around Fort Selkirk, built of logs and waving a Union Jack. There were hundreds of boats moored, and stalls and shops and a city of tents. But Fa wouldn't let them stop. 'Almost there now,' said Fa.

Those last days in the boat, Mr Stanley drank whisky quite often for his chill. He slept heavily, snoring loudly. His chin grew a dark beard and he smelled worse and worse. Ida was quite glad when a sudden downpour wetted them all.

'It's the only way Mr Stanley's going to take a wash,' she told Fa.

'We must just tolerate him until we reach Dawson,' said Fa.

Ida glanced across to where Mr Stanley stirred in his sleep, scratching his head of matted hair. Then she whispered to Fa, 'Are we not going to look for gold with him, then?'

'I think not,' said Fa. 'I've not told Stanley yet, mind you, so say nothing about it. But I feel that we shall fare better as a team of two, you and me. I've taken about as much as I can from that man, friend of your Uncle Stephen's or not.'

'Oh, good,' said Ida. She looked at Fa's tired eyes, the skin dark around them. 'Let me take a turn, Fa. You get some sleep.'

'Are you sure? I must confess, I can hardly keep my eyes open.'

Fa settled himself for a rest and Ida stood and steered, pulling and pushing the oar strapped to the back of the boat. She was wondering quite how the division of goods would be made between them and Mr Stanley, now that they were to go separate ways, when they rounded a rocky bluff and suddenly there was a rushing roaring dirty new river pouring into their Yukon from the right.

'It's . . . !' said Ida, shading her eyes and staring. 'It must be . . . oh, it's the Klondike River, at last!' And she burst into tears.

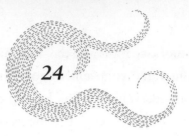

24

Beyond the Klondike River, dirty with mud, and maybe gold, there rose a tall pointed mountain with a raw, wounded-looking side. At the base of the mountain, sprawling over a huge marshy flat area, were thousands upon thousands of tents and shacks and cabins and warehouses, hotels, saloons and sawmills. The screech of timber being cut and hammering and shouting, all came at Ida as a shock. Hundreds of boats were already tied up at the muddy, swampy shoreline. They had arrived!

'Get up, Fa! We're here!'

Fa sat up, blinking.

'It's Dawson,' said Ida.

'Gracious!' said Fa, scrabbling to his feet and taking the steering oar from Ida. 'Grab the other oar, Stanley! We must paddle her in to land.' Except there was no clear place to land because so many boats were already there, jostling for position along Dawson's waterfront.

'We will have to tie alongside another boat,' said Fa. 'Good Lord, they are three or four deep! Hold tight to that other boat, Ida, or we'll be swept back into the river.'

They fought the current of the two combined rivers trying to push them on towards the sea, and they tied the

Isabella securely to a chunky square raft of a boat as the noise and smells and hustle from the bank swept over them in exciting waves.

'This is quite a place!' said Mr Stanley. 'Tell you what, Metcalf, why don't you and your lovely daughter go and take a look around? I'll guard the boat, so there'll be no need for you to fret about thieves or whatnot.' He waved a hand towards the bank. 'It might be an idea to hurry to the place where they sign papers to take a claim, don't you think? Before everyone else take the best sites? As I say, I'll hold the fort here, you purchase a claim, then we'll settle up in due course. Eh?'

Fa's eyes were sparkling . . . with tears, Ida realised. Ida had only ever seen Fa cry once, and that was when Mama died, and even then it was when he hadn't known that Ida was watching.

'Whatever is wrong?' she asked.

Fa threw out his arms. 'Nothing at all is wrong, my lovely Ida! Don't you see? We have made it, you and I! In spite of the doubters back home. In spite, truth be told, of my own doubts. We have come all this way, over all these months, and now the search for gold can begin. It's marvellous!'

'I can hardly stand,' laughed Ida, as she stood up on the boat and tried to straighten her grubby skirt. She felt somehow that she should try and look a little respectable for a visit to town, even if that town was made up mostly of tents and mud. She secretly slipped Duffle into a pocket, feeling he'd come so far with her that he should join her in landing on to Klondike earth. Then she stepped with Fa over the other boats to reach land at last, jumping ashore into thick mud. The land seemed to move. Ida grabbed Fa's arm.

'Sea legs,' laughed Fa. 'Or rather "river legs". It'll soon pass. Now, what should we do first? Can you see the claims office that Stanley was talking about?'

'There are proper buildings over that way,' said Ida.

But it wasn't easy to reach those buildings. Front Street was a strip of sloppy mud through which men were wandering, shuffling with bewildered expressions on their faces. It was hard to push through the crowd.

'Why aren't they setting off to find gold?' whispered Ida.

'I've no idea,' said Fa. 'What are they waiting for, I wonder?'

It was soon clear that many of those who had struggled for months, over mountains and down the Yukon, carrying their ton of goods, seemed to have lost any will to finally try and find gold. They were putting planks on top of boxes and selling off the goods they had carried so far. Boots and flour and oats and shovels and ground sheets and woollen long johns.

'Tinned peaches, soft and sweet!' somebody shouted.

'Those men are selling their outfits,' said Ida.

'To buy tickets to take them home,' said Fa. 'Quite astonishing.'

Fa walked fast, clutching Ida's hand. He gave the hand a little shake, then bent and spoke into her ear. 'This is good, Ida. Very good. All these chaps simply giving up without trying. That leaves the way clear for us!' Then Fa nudged Ida and nodded his head to point out a dapper little man, no taller than her. He was dressed in a finely tailored coat, shiny boots and a top hat. A jewelled tiepin glinted in the sunshine.

'I see you've spotted our Swiftwater Bill Gates!' said another man, leaning against a wooden store building. 'Gates has more money than he knows what to do with. Gold nuggets for buttons and drinks champagne for breakfast, and that's God's honest truth. Struck it rich and likes the world to know it.' The speaker was a hollow-cheeked man in clothes that were worn almost to bare threads.

'You've had no luck yourself?' said Fa.

The man guffawed. 'Oh, I've got gold.' He grinned at Fa. 'But I've got me something better and more lucky than gold now.' He waved a bit of paper at them.

'What could that be?' asked Fa.

The man did a little jig of a dance. 'This, Sir, English Man, is a ticket home to my wife and children. I'm off out of here, and I can't wait!'

'Well, we wish you well,' laughed Fa. 'Do you have any tips for newcomers?' Ida watched the man's eyes. Was he going to give them true advice or tricks?

'Well,' said the man, 'the cream of the pickings is all long gone. The milk of it is just about all gone too. There's still a chance for skimmed milk if you work your butt off day and night – er, pardon my language, Miss – but you'd do a whole lot better to get yourself an honest paid job in my opinion. Barber or dentist or somesuch. You ain't going to get rich looking for gold, and you'll very likely get poor.'

'So we're not too late if we're prepared to work hard,' said Fa. 'That's good to hear, especially when so many don't seem keen now that they've got here.'

They passed by rough wooden buildings with false fronts and painted signs: Opera House, Dance Hall, Lawyer, lots of Saloons, and . . .

'Look!' said Ida, pointing to a sign which read 'Gold dust bought and sold'. A line of men stood clutching jars and bags and bulging pockets, waiting their turn. Fa squeezed Ida's hand tight.

'You and I shall be in that queue with our poke of gold before you know it!'

'Excuse me Sir, Madam,' said a man. 'Are you newly arrived?'

'We are,' said Fa.

'Then can I interest you good people in buying a claim

rich in pay dirt that is for sale on remarkably reasonable terms?'

'You cannot,' said Fa firmly. 'Why in the world would anybody sell a site which is truly gold bearing at a cheap price when there are thousands of us pouring into town looking for that very thing? I simply don't believe you.' They walked away from the man.

'Can we find our own place instead of buying it here as Mr Stanley said we should?' asked Ida. 'Away from this town. And away from Mr Stanley too.'

'Yes,' said Fa. 'I reckon we should camp aboard the *Isabella* tonight, and settle things with Stanley tomorrow morning early, before setting out to find ourselves a place.' Fa kept talking plans as they turned and pushed their way through the crowd, back to the waterfront. 'We will need to buy some things if we are splitting what we have with Stanley. Fortunately for us, there are plenty eager to sell just about anything we might want, and at good prices, so we shan't lose too much that way.'

'Look how many more boats have arrived!' said Ida. They were six or seven deep now, moored to the waterfront.

'Remember what it said in the book?' said Fa, arms waving. 'There are nine thousand waterways in the region, so we can still be sure of finding something, if we're prepared to walk a little first.'

'Fa, where is the *Isabella*? I can't see her.'

A small steamship was coming upriver, and a crowd was pushing towards where it would dock.

'There's whisky aboard! Fresh eggs too! Maybe newspapers?'

The crowd was shouting and pushing, and it was hard to see the moored boats.

'She was just over . . . er, she must be hidden behind the steamship.'

They searched up and down the waterfront, and up and down again. But neither Mr Stanley nor the *Isabella* were there.

2 July 1898

Dear Grandmama,

I hope that this letter finds you well. Fa and I are well in body, so you must not worry, but we have had a very great setback. I shall try to tell you about it in a way which doesn't alarm too much. Fa is to travel back to Dawson today, to sign the papers that must be signed before we can own the claim we have found, and he can post this letter whilst he is there. I know that you would rather receive a letter on fine paper, and written with the pen you gave me, but perhaps you will understand once I have explained things.

In my last letter I told you how we had got a Mr

Stanley with us for the river journey to Dawson. Well, we completed the river trip, with some adventures which I will tell you about when I get home. We arrived in Dawson with all well. There were such crowds of men there! Yet many of them have already given up any hope of finding gold, and simply want to go home. But Fa is a determined man. So, we have found ourselves a place to dig for gold, and will work hard to succeed in that.

So, as you can see, we are set on our course for gold and about to begin the search. But this comes after a great misfortune. Mr Stanley has disappeared, and he has stolen from us. He was not a gentleman after all, for all that he told us that he is Uncle Stephen's friend. I think that Uncle Stephen should choose his friends more carefully, for Mr Stanley is a thief and a liar, and I hate him with a loathing I never thought I would ever feel for anybody. I am sorry to say it, but the truth is that I would like to hurt him, because he has hurt Fa and me. But Fa somehow forgives and blames himself for believing Mr Stanley in the first place. That makes me want to punch Fa too, but of course I do not because he is upset and it wouldn't be fair.

Mr Stanley has taken our Isabella boat and all that was in her, which was just about everything. All those cases and sacks and crates of goods which Fa and I had carried over the mountains and down the river – all gone. The saddest loss of all, to me, is the brooch which had belonged to Mama, and which Fa gave me at Christmas. The beautiful pen you gave me is also gone. And the money which we were keeping especially for good or bad times later. And the tools and tent and, oh, so much!

Fa reported the theft, but was told that in such a place there is practically no hope of getting anything back. Likely, Mr Stanley is on a steamboat and quite away already. I don't think that he ever truly intended to work for gold. You will be glad to know that clever Fa kept some money safe in a money belt around his waist, rather than in the boat. With so many people selling their outfits and heading for home it has been easy to buy tools and food, but we have less than we did of both. Perhaps that is as well because we could not have carried all our goods at once.

Fa and I took what we could on our backs and left Dawson. We travelled like tinkers, with pots dangling and clanking as we walked in search of a claim. Fa said we made our own percussion band. I think that my aunts would not approve of that, but I hope that you see that is just how things have to be out here.

The valleys around are full of miners working

the ground and the streams, looking for gold. Your Mr Smith in the garden would be upset to see how so many trees have been cut down for fuel and for building cabins and water runs. Much of the ground is so dug and scraped that it is all a mess of stumps and mud and humps of pay dirt waiting to be washed. There are rough dens for living in, and broken jars and rags and tins, and even graves, where there should be beautiful plants and peace. There is a strange sad sighing sound, that never stops, coming from hundreds upon hundreds of windlasses drawing buckets up from the earth. The weather is so hot now that the damp places swarm with mosquitoes. Many miners are struck with fever and ague, but Fa and I use netting at night to stop the worst of the mosquito bites, so we have not suffered that illness yet.

We walked many miles, up into hills and further and further until the mining places were fewer and farther apart, but they also yield less gold, we are told. 'Never mind,' says Fa. He says that he will work twice as hard as other miners, so will get the same from a claim that yields only half as much gold in its soil. I will work hard too. There are not so very many weeks before the short summer here is over and winter closes in once more. So we must use these long days that are hardly broken by the brief darkness around midnight.

But I haven't yet told you where we shall be living and working. We have found a little cabin home on a claim of land, both of which have been deserted. It has a name, burned by hot poker onto a piece of wood. It is called Little Eldorado. Our neighbours, Mr and Mrs McKenzie, tell us that the previous owners of the claim found some gold on the surface, but had no further luck when they dug, so they left after the winter, thinking there was no more gold to be found, but Fa thinks otherwise. He is disinclined to trust what anybody tells him after the way that Mr Stanley and others have treated us. He says that the McKenzies would say that there was no gold because they want to keep any gold around here for themselves. They seem to have very little. I would not blame them if they did want more.

So we are trying our luck here. We will have a home of our own once Fa has filed the proper papers to make it all legal. In our cabin we have a stove and a table that were already here. We even have a window, so we feel quite grand after our months of living in a tent.

Now Fa is to walk fast back to Dawson to register his name on Little Eldorado. Mrs McKenzie has said that I can eat and sleep with them while Fa is away, which is kind of her, I think. There are bears in these hills. Mama would have liked Mrs

McKenzie. She is fat and smiley, and she takes the trouble to put flowers in a jam jar to brighten their cabin, even though she is so busy washing the soil that her husband digs.

Think how wonderful it would be if I could find gold to surprise Fa with when he returns from Dawson. I won't tell that wish to Fa, only to you just now, but I will try a little panning while he is away. It is strange to think that by the time you read this, we may, I pray, have found gold and fulfilled our quest. Next time I write I hope that it will be with news of that golden find.

With love to you, and my regards to my cousins and aunts,

Your loving,

Ida

25

'You mind you don't go falling down any of them holes! We don't want no broken bones!' warned Mrs McKenzie as Ida carried the bundle of her rough blanket and pillow towards the path to the McKenzie cabin.

There were three big holes in the ground around the cabin on Little Eldorado and soil piled beside those holes. Mrs McKenzie nodded towards them and told Ida, 'Those fellas at your place worked as hard as any, but they never did find a pay streak, in spite of digging and digging all through winter, then rinsing and washing when the streams thawed. Not a fleck of gold in the whole darn pile.'

'But have you found gold on your claim?' asked Ida, wondering, as she said it, if it was rude to ask a question about wealth.

'Some,' said Mrs McKenzie. 'Enough to stop sense that would have told us to give up on the whole damn thing! But not enough to live on. Not enough to see us through another winter, unless some miracle brings us fine big nuggets in the weeks left to us before the fall.' She shook her head and turned down the path. As she swung around she pushed a hand into her back in a way that Ida suddenly recognised.

'Oh!'

'What's that?' asked Mrs McKenzie.

'Um, I . . . oh . . . excuse me, but are you going to have a baby?' asked Ida.

Mrs McKenzie smiled wide.

'Why, yes I am,' she said. 'Though the good Lord only knows how we'll manage once we've a small one, and me likely too busy to help my husband, Nathan.'

'I can help,' said Ida, as they walked over to the McKenzie cabin.

'You know what, Miss Metcalf?' said Mrs McKenzie. 'You already have, by cheering me with your company. Why, I think it's going to be nice for me having a girl such as yourself for a neighbour.'

'Please call me Ida,' said Ida. 'That's my name.'

'Well, I'm Carrie,' said Mrs McKenzie, and Ida realised that Carrie probably wasn't very much beyond just being a girl herself.

So the six days it took for Fa to get to Dawson and back were quite happy ones for Ida. They were days in which she learnt how to make griddle scones and how to wash the piles of soil, or 'dirt', that Nathan McKenzie had dug.

Nathan had diverted water from the creek to run through a series of sluice boxes he'd built. Carrie and Ida loaded the mud into those sluice boxes and watched as it was washed down. After hours of loading and sluicing, Nathan diverted the water from the box and told Ida to take a look at what was left in the bottom.

'Rocks and mud,' she said.

'Look again,' said Nathan. 'Look in the fine dark mud caught right under all else.'

'Oh!' Ida pointed, and a strange feeling surged through her. There were specs of gold dust, glinting amongst the dark grit caught in the rough hessian cloth at the bottom of the box. 'Is that truly gold?'

'It is,' agreed Nathan. 'Now we have to get that gold dust out of the heavy dirt.'

Ida's heart was thumping hard in her chest. 'How do we do that?'

'Well, that black sludge there is magnetite – iron ore. We use a magnet to get that away from the gold.'

They showed Ida how to wrap a magnet in a rag, then run it through the damp sludge to pick up all the ore. Then take the rag from the magnet and rinse the ore off it. The pinch of gold dust left at the end of this long operation was pitifully small, even to Ida's excited view.

'Only worth a few cents,' said Nathan with a shrug. But it is real gold, thought Ida. And there must surely be more waiting to be found.

At supper, Ida asked, 'Mr McKenzie, could I pan for gold in the creek? Would I find any there?'

'You'll find nothing worth the labour of panning,' said Nathan. 'We've all tried it many a time. The only pickings worth working for around here are in the ground and have to be dug for.'

So the plan that Ida had written to Grandmama about wasn't going to work.

After lunch of corned beef and pickle on crackers, eaten on tree stumps out in the sunshine, Nathan went back to his sluice boxes and Carrie asked Ida, 'You want to help with the kind of washing that produces more gold than Nathan's big box there ever will?'

'What sort of washing is that?' asked Ida. 'And, if it's better than Nathan's kind, why don't you and he just do that sort all the time?'

Carrie laughed. 'Because I've got myself a man who has a pride that gives him a need to prove something to himself, and to the world, that's why. A bit like your pa, from what little I've seen of him. But you and me, Ida, we got sense to see what needs to be done, and then to damn well do it. And what that is, is washing the filthy stinking clothes of those men who haven't brought their wives or daughters along with them and who ain't inclined to learn domestic skills.'

'You're a washerwoman?' said Ida.

'I am. And so are you this afternoon, if you'll help me.'

So Ida went with Carrie, off into the woods and along the creeks, collecting mostly shirts and long pants and handkerchiefs and socks from men working claims all around. Ida's job was to write down names of men and descriptions of garments so that they would all get their own clothes back once they'd been cleaned. Ida stuffed the items into a big sack, holding it away from her as she did so.

'Told you they smelled bad!' laughed Carrie. She swung the full sack over her back.

'You look like Father Christmas,' said Ida.

'Fine sort of presents for good children these stinky socks and pants would make!' laughed Carrie. 'We'll put them all in to soak, then boil up the water to wash them in tomorrow morning. If the rain holds off they'll dry before the next day, then we can take them all back to their owners.'

'And get paid?'

'That's the idea. I certainly don't do it for love of washing. Why don't you go fetch the things that you and your pa need freshening and we'll throw them in along with the rest.'

Ida hurried back to Little Eldorado. It looked a damp dingy hovel of a place now that Ida compared it with the McKenzie home, which was no bigger, but was cared for. She looked at the piles of dull dirt around the cabin, with not a spark of gold glinting in the soil that she could see. What if there really isn't any gold in any of our dirt? What if Fa is spending our very last money to buy this place and it's no good? What if something happens to Fa in Dawson and he doesn't come back?

Ida snatched up the very few bits of clothing she and Fa weren't wearing. She took Fa's blanket too. It could be washed and dried by the time he came home. She must try and make a home of this place, as Carrie had done at her cabin. And maybe she too would have to find ways of making money that didn't depend on finding gold, if finding gold was so very hard.

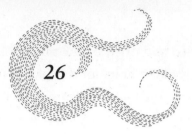

26

Ida and Carrie dragged buckets of water from the stream and heated the water in pans on Carrie's stove. Ida brought wood to feed the fire, but Carrie insisted on lifting the heavy steaming pans of water to pour them into the tin bath.

'Should you be doing that?' asked Ida, looking at Carrie's bulging belly.

'Maybe I should, maybe I shouldn't,' said Carrie. 'But I ain't got no maid to call on to do it for me.'

'I can help,' said Ida, reaching for a pan, but Carrie put a hand on her arm.

'No you don't, thank you all the same. What I can't be doing with is somebody injured with a scalding. I've no clean dressings and no time for invalids. Judging by the kicking he's doing, this baby don't mind a bit of work. So that's a good sign for the future.'

'Could I feel?' asked Ida. Carrie took her hand and placed it to one side of her belly. There was a pause, when Ida felt nothing, and then – bump! – she was firmly kicked.

'Oh!' laughed Ida. 'Goodness.' She tried to imagine the baby, curled up inside the dark warmth of its mother. Hard to think that she, Ida, had been inside dainty Mama like that at one time.

They plunged the dirty clothes into the heated water. It was so hot it made their hands red and their faces sweat. They used sticks to stir the clothes, but the water soon cooled enough to allow them to rub the clothes with hard rough soap.

'Think of all the things that make you feel that life ain't fair. That'll help you treat the clothes good and rough, and that'll get that dirt out,' advised Carrie. The bending down with her full belly made her back ache, so soon it was Ida who was doing most of the work as Carrie eased her back and strung up ropes from trees for a washing line.

Ida thought of the Reverend Bowers as she pummelled a plaid shirt with tight fists. She thought of Mr Stanley as she wrung out a pair of trousers, twisting them hard. Ida thought of her cousins as she slapped a pair of socks against the sides of the tin bath. Squeeze, hit, bash.

'Well, I sure don't want to get on the wrong side of you!' laughed Carrie. 'You're doing good.'

Ida's arms ached and she was wet with both sweat and splashes of water by the time they'd washed the clothes and Fa's heavy blanket. They rinsed away the dirty soapy water by taking the heavy tin bath, full of sodden clothes, to the stream, where they let the cold stream water take the soap and dirt off and away. Ida's arms ached with all the wringing out she'd done, as at last they hung the clothes.

'Not the finest Fourth of July bunting,' said Carrie,

contemplating the flapping rags of clothes, 'but clean, at least.' She smiled. 'And done a whole lot sooner, and easier, for having you to help. I thank you, Ida.'

When Fa came back Ida was in Little Eldorado, trying to make a home of the place. Ida heard his shout:

'Is a Miss Metcalf in residence?'

'Fa!' She ran outside into his arms and clung tight.

'Steady on!' laughed Fa. 'Goodness, did you think that I wouldn't come back?' Ida didn't answer that. She felt a strange mix of wanting to haul Fa inside and make him some tea and get him to tell his news, and an almost equally strong urge to thump him hard for having been gone so long and scaring her. Fa looked around the cabin and waved an arm to encompass it all,

'You've made a palace of the place!'

Ida had used a bunch of leaves to sweep the dried mud floor. She had dragged in logs to be stools beside the table. She had made mattresses by filling sheeting bags with dried grass, then covered them with the blankets with hospital corners tucked in.

'Welcome home, Fa,' she smiled.

Fa had brought what he could carry in the way of supplies. 'Our old friends, the bean and the rice grain, plus a big sack of flour and tins of condensed milk, which I suggest we save for celebrating when we strike it rich. They were a shocking price, but I bought two tins – one to be a present for the McKenzies as thanks for their caring for you.'

'The McKenzies are nice,' said Ida. 'Really kind. And Carrie is expecting a baby.'

'Excellent. I think that this place is going to do us very well. All we have to do now is to work it and find that gold.' That was the start of what would become two hot and humid months of gruelling work for Ida and Fa.

Little Eldorado

25 August 1898

My dear Grandmama,
I hope that this finds you very well.

I feel sure that you must be wondering whether or not we have yet found gold. We have! If you have opened this letter carefully, you will have seen one fine flake of real Klondike gold enfolded within the top corner. I know that you have a quantity of golden jewellery of your own, but I thought that you might like to see some gold the way that it is in the wild. We have not yet found gold nuggets nor made our fortune, but we live in hope.

Our neighbour Mr Nathan McKenzie is to do the long walk to Dawson to buy supplies and he has offered to take this letter to the mail post whilst he is there. A great thunderstorm, raining and rumbling and flashing outside, has put an end to washing clothes or washing soil for the moment, and so that gives me the time in which to write to you. I wonder if any of my letters have reached you at the big house? It seems such a very long way away from here. When the weather gets so very hot and humid and full of mosquitoes, I long to sit in your garden, sheltered from the sun under the big willow tree, to drink lemonade and eat those tiny cucumber sandwiches, and to know that nothing much needs to be done.

Here we are busy every moment of light. I am almost glad that the days are shortening again because I find myself so tired by the time darkness stops our work. It is not quite true that work stops when darkness comes. There are always tools to be sharpened and clothes to be mended by candlelight. I worry that Fa does not rest enough. He is so very determined to work all he may before winter comes.

Let me describe our life now. The days here are very hot. Vegetation of all sorts is blooming all around. I have some briar roses in a tin can beside me, and there are plenty of salmonberries and blueberries to be made into tasty pies, or even sauces for meat when we get some (moose steaks which we buy from a hunter if we have the money). I have learnt from my friend and neighbour Mrs Carrie

McKenzie how to make soap out of bear fat and lye (ashes). Her husband, Nathan, shot a bear, so for a short while there was a great deal of bear meat to eat. The shame is that the weather was too humid to allow the meat to be dried, so much of it was given away or sold to other miners.

The bear fat is used for making soap and candles. We used it to grease our hands when Carrie and I made toffee as a surprise for Nathan on his birthday. We boiled molasses, then cooled and tugged and twisted the mixture, then doubled-up and twisted it again until the toffee was soft. I was also able to use the bear fat to waterproof Fa's and my boots, which have become very worn and shoddy. The great pelt of fur from the bear will help keep Nathan and Carrie warm this coming winter.

Fa has tried so many ways to get gold. He digs and washes endlessly on our own claim, but that has yielded very little. It seems very unfair after all the work, but he has hopes of finding more if he can dig deep enough. If only there was a sure way to know whether or not more gold is there to be found. Fa met a Welshman, Mr Edwards, who said that he came from a gold-mining family and that he could taste stream water and know at once whether it bore gold or not. I fed Mr Edwards a good supper using our evaporated vegetables and sugar, which we keep *only for special occasions, and Mr Edwards stayed the night. He tasted our creek water and said that the creek was a rich one, which was strange when we have found nothing. Fa even paid a lady clairvoyant who came travelling in the area. She also said she was able to tell where gold would or would not be found. She assured Fa that our claim was a good one. That cheered him once more and set him working harder than ever. But I wonder why these people who say that they know so much are not themselves rich with gold finds? You would, I think, be very proud of Fa for working so hard and for not drinking whisky or gambling with cards as many miners do.*

Fa is digging at a great depth and that is horrid work. He has talked to other miners and is sure that fifteen feet is the depth where gold will be found. The people who worked this claim before did not go so deep and Fa says that was their mistake and our good fortune. But it has taken over six weeks to achieve that depth, which is, after all, more than twice Fa's own height. With Mr McKenzie's help, Fa has built a frame over the hole so that buckets of soil may be winched up, and Fa himself may be winched up and down the hole. I worry that rains like the present storm might come when I am away from the claim and he has nobody to call for help; then who will winch him out before the hole fills with water?

We keep testing the soil, washing it in the wooden sluice box that Fa bought from a miner who was heading home. The exciting, but worrying, days are when we stop the water from going through the sluice to see if any gold has been trapped. Sometimes we see the glitter of flakes of gold (like the one in this letter) caught in the rough hessian. Then we do a little dance before we carefully collect every speck that we can. Often there is no gold at all, and then it is hard not to be downcast at having worked so very hard for no reward. But one of us will say that we are sure to have better luck next time, and on we go.

Fa works all of every day, except for Sundays. Every night Fa, and all the other miners around, set fires to burn in their diggings, making the whole area full of smoke and stench. Even in our hot daytime weather, the earth below the top two or three feet is still frozen, so needs to be thawed before it can be worked. We have already had a night frost. Winter is coming again to freeze it all. We will surely find Fa's gold soon.

I have written at great length and in what my teacher would have called 'a ramble'. I hope that it doesn't bore you. Fa sends regards, as do I, to all at the big house, but especially to you.

Your loving granddaughter,
Ida Metcalf

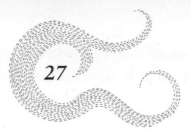

27

What Ida didn't tell Grandmama was how very worried she was about Fa. He worked so hard that he was too tired to eat properly. He was so tired that he often lay straight down on his bed and fell asleep without even taking his boots off. Ida would remove his battered boots and place a blanket over him, and hope to feed him a good breakfast the next morning. Fa had become so very thin that you could see every bone in his hands and even see the shape of his skull behind the beard that had grown very long again. When he stood, he was stooped like an old man. Ida also worried that Fa was becoming ill in his mind as well as his body.

'This damn land is fighting me every inch of the way!' he said. It wasn't like Fa to swear, and Fa's anger at the land as some kind of personal enemy grew daily until he came up with a startling suggestion. Arms waving, he told Ida, 'It has become clear to me that this land wants something from us before it will give anything back.' It has already taken your health, thought Ida, but that wasn't what Fa had in mind. 'We must make the land an offering: give it something in exchange for the gold and then, I feel, it will release the gold to us.'

'But what could we give it?' asked Ida.

'Oh, food or . . . or something precious, because gold is precious, do you see? It's an exchange. Only fair, when you think about it.'

So they buried the tin of condensed milk in the Klondike mud.

But nothing changed.

Fa went on working himself to exhaustion. He cut himself badly, stepping onto his rusty shovel with a bare foot when washing himself, and the cut turned bad. Ida bathed and bandaged it, but the swelling worked up and up Fa's leg, red and hot and swollen. Ida got Carrie to look at it.

'Reckon that needs seeing by a man who knows medicine,' she said. But a doctor would cost money.

'We can't afford one. I'll do without,' said Fa, rocking back and forth to cope with the pain. Days and nights of fever followed, with Fa shivering and sweating, getting even thinner and saying strange things in his semi-sleep. It looked to Ida as though Fa might die so she looked through all his pockets and all the places where she thought he might be keeping some money hidden. After all, he had promised to keep back enough to take them home again.

But there was no money anywhere except the cents that Ida had earned from the washing, and that wasn't anywhere near enough to pay for a doctor. No money for a doctor. No money for going home. Ida prayed. 'Give us this day our daily bread,' she recited, and she meant every word of that in a way she never had back in England where there was always at least bread to eat. She fed Fa sloppy gruels made with leaves that Carrie suggested, then gentle foods to try and tempt his appetite back. And, slowly, the leg began to heal. So too did Fa's sense of humour. He put on a Grandmama voice.

'I'm ill,' he said. 'But not as ill as I look.'

Too soon, Fa was back down his hole, digging for gold.

Ida hadn't told Grandmama in the letter that the money that kept them in beans and rice and sugar and salt nearly all now came from her own small earnings from helping Carrie with the laundry. Carrie had shown Ida where to find food for free too, picking leaves and berries and digging roots to add taste to the boring beans, rice and bacon. The bear meat had been a welcome change. Ida remembered Mama saying, 'there's nothing like good fresh food to restore health'. It hadn't worked for Mama herself, but now Ida fed Fa fresh food whenever she could afford the time away from the washing of dirt and clothes to go looking for it.

She liked the excuse, walking into the wilds where she could forget about gold for a time. Although, even then, gold was never far from her thoughts. She watched ravens pecking at a carcass and thought of how they were like magpies and would steal bright things. Could ravens be trained to pick bright specks of gold from dirt? Had anybody tried that? Mostly Ida just wished that Fa could be persuaded to come with her on her walks. It would do him good to get beyond the mining district, she was sure.

Ida came back from one foraging walk to find Fa sat on a log with his head in his hands. Ida put her arms around him. She knew that it wasn't his leg that was troubling him this time.

'Is it so very bad?' she said.

'Very bad indeed,' said Fa, then he laughed a little strangely and looked at her. 'In fact, my dear, it is the end of hope. I have dug that damned hole a good four foot deeper than the fifteen feet I was assured would take me to the pay streak and I've found no gold at all in the last five foot. Nothing but frozen mud . . . and this morning, I hit solid rock. Even the pick hardly chips a dent in it.' He lifted empty hands. 'What should I do, Ida? Keep chipping away until I reach the centre of the earth? Or give up?' He sighed deeply and shook his head. 'There simply is no gold to be found here beyond the tease of a few flakes,' he said. 'That is the truth of the matter.'

'I know,' said Ida.

Fa look at her and smiled sadly. 'Yes. You have known a long time what your foolish Fa has taken weeks to discover. So, my clever daughter, tell me, what are we to do now? I'm out of ideas, and out of money.'

Ida's heart jolted nastily in her chest as she heard Fa admit that he really had spent every bit of the money from

Grandmama that hadn't been stolen. She felt strangely adrift and trapped. We can't stay and we can't escape! Ida pushed her hair back behind her ears, and sat down to face Fa. 'Carrie says that if she gave up her laundry business, then she and Nathan would soon go hungry. What you and I need, Fa, is a business like Carrie's.'

'Doing washing?'

'No, that's Carrie's business and we are not going to take it from her. We must think of some new kind of business or service that nobody else is doing out here yet. Something the mining men who have found gold will pay for.'

Fa tugged at his beard. 'But what, that's the question?'

Ida's mind scrabbled for ideas, her eyes darted around the cabin, looking for inspiration. The sack in which she'd collected berries and leaves and roots was by the doorway.

'Pies,' she said. 'There are lots of berries to be picked just now. The strawberries are over, but there are still blueberries and salmonberries and cranberries. We still have a sack of flour for sourdough crust, and molasses and some sugar, even some spices and dried vinegar. We can sell pies to the miners.'

'Well, it can't do any worse than my mining, I don't suppose,' said Fa.

So Ida took Fa berry picking. She set him to work washing and topping and tailing the berries, and chopping logs for the stove. She sent him to the McKenzies to borrow Carrie's pie tins. By early afternoon there were five glistening, juicy, sweet blueberry, mint and molasses pies cooling on their table. It was Fa who thought of adding wild mint to the fruit. He wiped a hand over his forehead.

'This is hard work!' he said. 'You know, I'm almost longing for the coolness to be found down . . .'

'. . . down your damned hole?' said Ida, giving him a look. But it was good to hear him laugh.

They took the fresh pies, covered with clean cloths, down the valley to the miners. Fa looked funny carrying pies, his exhausted face concentrating hard on not dropping one. 'Well, partner,' he said. 'I suppose this is where we test your new enterprise.'

The first mine they visited was run by a group of five men who Ida already knew from her visits with Carrie.

'My, that is a sight for sore eyes!' said Mr Mulroony, throwing down his shovel, wiping muddy hands on his breeches, and taking his hat off in a gallant gesture to Ida. 'I've not clapped eyes on fresh baking since, oh, weeks back when I paid a fortune for nothing very much in Dawson. I'll take three of those good-looking pies, and happy to pay for them.'

'I will be back for the dishes and then I can bring more' said Ida. Then she frowned. 'Oh, but I won't have any dishes to cook the next pies in.'

'We can make dishes,' said Fa, his grey face animated with excitement. 'I've seen old tin cans flattened and shaped into pie dishes, and there are plenty of cans around here.' He pointed to the pile of empty food cans that the miners had dumped. 'We wouldn't even need to collect those back after we'd sold the pies.'

'You're more than welcome to help yourselves to anything from that pile of garbage. And bring more pies any time you have any,' said Mr Mulroony.

So they filled the basket with dirty old tin cans, being careful not to cut themselves on the sharp edges.

The next site was run by a pair of brothers, but they had six other men working for them.

'How's two pies going to be enough for eight of us?' asked Big Dennis.

'We'll bring more next time,' said Ida.

'In that case, me and my brother will test out these two samples here, and you can bring more next time if we like them.' Big Dennis looked at Fa. 'Canny idea of yours, setting your gal to cooking.'

Fa smiled, and Ida didn't tell that Fa had shared in the cooking, or that the idea had been hers.

Big Dennis's mine had machines, run by creek water, to dig and wash in a noisy, dirty operation that was eating more and more of the valley sides, and messing the creek.

'Are you finding good pay dirt?' asked Fa.

'Yep. Found a good rich streak,' said Big Dennis. 'Only thing is, we need to work fast to get all the gold we can before winter sets in. We've all promised our folks that we'll be home this fall, so we're flat out now to take what we can before we leave. Say, we could do with the extra labour if you're willing and available?'

'Um, well I hadn't . . .' Fa fiddled with his beard. 'Labouring is not something I had thought of doing, but . . .'

'How much do you pay your men?' asked Ida, and both men laughed.

'I see that she's your business manager, as well as cook general, huh?' said the man. 'I pay what's fair for fair work, that's what I pay. How does eighty dollars a month sound?' He glanced at Fa's calloused hands. 'You look a worker, but you speak like a gent. Can you labour?'

In jumped Ida again. 'Fa works harder than anybody else in this whole valley.'

Big Dennis chuckled. 'Well, your little lady's recommendation is good enough for me, Metcalf. Be here early tomorrow and we'll take it from there.'

Fa was quiet as they walked home, the coins they'd taken in payment clinking in his pocket and the dirty old tin cans clanking gently in the basket.

'It will be good to work for a wage and know that you will be paid at the end of the day,' Ida told him.

Fa sighed. 'You are right, of course. But I am now a hired hand,' he said. 'And you, my love, are a washerwoman's help and pie-maker. Whatever would Mama have thought?'

'She'd be proud,' said Ida firmly.

Ida felt almost as if Fa was her child, and she was sending him off to school, as she checked that he had a clean shirt and a handkerchief all ready for an early start at his new job in the morning.

'It's labouring,' said Fa. 'A clean shirt won't stay clean.' He straightened his tie and shrugged his worn tweed jacket over his shoulders. The other miners mostly wore jerseys, but Fa was never parted from his jacket. 'Keeps me warm in the cold, and cools me in the heat,' he said. So Fa set off looking bedraggled, but an English gentleman none the less.

It was strange being alone on the claim without Fa. Ida busied herself with washing tin cans, soaking off the food labels, then hammering them flat before working the edges, tapping around the rim against a stone to give each small dish a lip. By the end of the day she had a pile of shiny clean patty pans ready for pies.

Through September Ida's days took on a pattern. On Mondays she worked with Carrie, collecting and washing dirty garments and linen. Tuesday was for folding and delivering the cleaned stuff. Wednesday she went collecting berries or soaking dried apples that she had bought. Thursdays were for baking and delivering pies, hot and fresh from the oven. Fridays were spent making more pie tins. And by the weekend Ida had a satisfying collection of small coins jingling in her pockets. On Saturdays she made Little Eldorado clean and pleasant and cooked bread and stews to last through the next week. Maybe Fa and I can make a living here after all, she thought. They were earning just enough for the two of them to live on now, but Ida knew it couldn't last. Winter wasn't far away. Already the berries were almost all gone, so Ida was having to buy dried fruit for her pies and that made the profit on the pies less. The number of miners wanting clothes washed had gone down too.

'More and more of 'em heading back home,' said Carrie.

The flour bag sagged, almost empty. If Ida was to go on making pies, they would have to spend more of her earnings on ingredients. The cost of supplies was bound to go up as the river froze out steamships. Maybe supplies would stop altogether. Then what?

Then Fa lost his job. He came home at midday as Ida was sitting beside the stove, sewing flour bags stuffed with rags together to make a quilt to try and keep Fa warmer in bed. Fa looked a kind of ghost, grey and skeletal and coughing, and he sat down heavily on his bed.

'Fa?'

Fa delved into his jacket pocket and took out a handful of coins which he held out for Ida. 'That is all of it and an end of it,' he said. 'An end to my labouring for other men. I can't say that I'm sad to see the back of that job.'

'But, Fa . . . ?'

'Big Dennis said that he was cutting payment to just two meals of beans and bacon a day and nothing more.

No real pay at all. There are men desperate enough to agree to such terms.' Fa waved his arms. 'I know, I know, my love. We are fairly desperate ourselves.' Fa coughed into a dirty handkerchief. 'But the truth of it is . . .' Fa shook his head, 'that I am simply too tired to carry on.' He lay down, closed his eyes and muttered, 'I know that I am a poor sort of a Fa to you, my dear. A poor sort of a man altogether.'

'No! You are a fine man and a fine Fa!' insisted Ida, stroking and then patting Fa's back. 'Don't worry, Fa. All will be well, I'm sure that it will.'

But she wasn't sure at all.

Fa fell straight to sleep, but it was a troubled sleep that had him whimpering and twitching. As a cold dawn lightened outside, Ida slipped out of bed and stoked up the stove, as much to heat the cabin as to boil coffee. Fa eased himself out of bed, pale and gaunt, and he sat to sip at the coffee.

'I have been thinking of a plan,' he said.

'You were muttering in the night,' said Ida.

'There's a place called Nome, up in the north-west.' Fa pointed over his shoulder as if Nome were just around the corner and not hundreds of miles away. 'There's gold mixed into the beach sands there. Soft easy digging, so if we were to go and . . .'

'No, Fa!' Ida stamped. 'No! You are ill and it is almost winter. And I don't believe there would be easy pickings in any case!' Ida was shaking with fury and fright. 'You said that there would be gold here on this claim, didn't you? Hmm? Remember, you said there was gold when Mr Edwards tasted gold in the water? You said that by praying hard, and by giving presents to the land, we would get gold. Well none of that got us enough gold to live on and neither did hard work!' Ida waved her arms, Fa-style. 'There never was any gold beyond a few crumbs, so we are not, not, not going chasing another place that you say will certainly have gold!' Ida looked at Fa's ill helpless face. It was terrifying. So she ran. Out of the cabin, away from Fa's hurt, away from their failure. Away.

28

Ida ran from the claim, but there was no escape from her thoughts. *No money to take us home. No money to let us survive a winter here. Fa is going to die, just as Mama did, unless I can save him, but I don't know how!*

Ida ran uphill. Above her the sky rolled with churning dark clouds and the day heated to a fuggy humidity. Ida's boots were soon sodden by the spongy, mossy ground that seemed to suck and cling to her feet.

'Let me go!'

Midges smudged and bumped the muggy air in a cloud around her head. Ida swatted at them as she went. She picked up a stick to swish through the air and swash away the grasses that tried to tangle her. Sobbing and running, tears blurring her vision, Ida stumbled on. She had no idea where she was going, just away.

As the ground became steeper, and her legs tired, Ida slowed to a climbing walk. The land was dryer and the air cooler above the main valley, the flies and midges fewer. There was a breeze that filled Ida's lungs with fresh air and seemed to clear her mind a little. She was up in the mountains now, above the mining settlements with their scarred ground so hacked and spoiled by shovels and picks and fires. She was above the streams that were dammed and stirred and muddied by miners. She was above all the hurt that men had done to the land.

Looking around at lush unspoilt beauty, Ida felt a stir of sympathy for the Klondike land. Up here the trees were proper trees, not ugly stumps. They were tall and branched, leaved in crimsons, purples, oranges and greens, turning autumnal in their colouring. Fa should come up here and paint this, thought Ida. If only Fa had paints. If only Fa had time and strength. If only he were proper Fa again. Ida twisted to look all around.

And that was when she saw the bear.

The bear was a big grizzly one, standing huge on its back legs like a giant man in a fur coat. It was looking down its long nose, straight at Ida. Ida's insides seemed to slip, making her feel strangely faint and cold and clammy. Her heart banged like a blacksmith's hammer, and the hair on the back of her head seemed to creep.

She had heard talk about bears. They like to eat you alive, chewing your buttocks or legs, then leaving you wounded before coming back for more. They can run faster than a person, and climb trees better than a person. So how can you escape?

Ida remembered Carrie saying that the way to avoid trouble with bears was to make plenty of noise when you were in bear territory, because bears will avoid humans if they can. But Ida had been quiet. And now the grizzly was as startled to see her as she was to see it.

'I-I'm sorry, Bear,' she said, rather stupidly. She swallowed hard and began to back away from the bear. 'Sorry for being in your place. Sorry for what we have done to your land. Sorry . . .' She went on talking, all the time keeping eye contact with the bear, all the time slowly backing away. The bear reached out a hairy arm that ended squarely with huge, spiked black claws. Ida held her breath, closed her eyes, and waited for the bear to pounce and those claws to strike.

But the bear didn't come.

Ida counted in her head. One, two, three . . . she peeked out of half-open eyes to see the bear reach a terribly clawed paw . . . up to a bunch of berries. It posted the berries into its mouth and chewed in a thoughtful way.

'Huh!' Ida breathed out a sob of relief. She stepped away again now, quietly, carefully, then turning and going faster until she was running, stumbling. She glanced over her shoulder as she ran from the bear towards a line of trees, where she thought she could at least hide behind a tree trunk, but . . . trip! Her foot twisted in a root and she fell crashing down to lie flat on the grass. Her ankle screaming in pain, Ida froze still and listened for the thump thump thump of a bounding heavy bear.

But all she could hear was birds singing, her own laboured breathing and blood thumping in her ears. She smelled the damp dank earth. She heard the breeze rustling the trees nearby, strangely comfortingly, like waves on the pebble beach back at home. Ida twisted her head and slowly looked up to see that something tall was looming over her. But it wasn't a bear. It was a tree umbrellaed over her, its bright orange leaves vivid against a dark grey sky and spoked by dark branches.

Ida pushed down on the grassy earth to get herself into a crouching position. She looked around. The bear wasn't there. Ida breathed out and realised that her fist was clutching a clump of grassy earth that she must have grabbed and held on to when she fell. She opened her hand to let the soil fall, then saw something blinking, warm and yellow from amongst the soily roots of that grass.

'Gold?'

Three golden nuggets, round and wobbly-shaped as raisins. Ida moved her hand and the nuggets clunked together with a soft sound. They were heavy in her hand. Real.

'Gold!'

Ida clasped a fist around the nuggets, then bent and pulled more grass away from the rock, uncovering sandy soil in which gold nuggets nestled like new potatoes for the picking. Laughing, Ida filled the pockets on either side of her skirt, liking the heavy feel of her golden harvest. And under that sandy, nugget-rich layer of soil and grass there was another kind of richness; a grey, crystalline granite kind of rock, but with a great streak of gold spilling through it. Solid, but looking liquid within the jagged sharp rock.

'Gracious!'

Ida bent down to claw away more grass and soil. The streak of gold ran thickly in some places, thinly in others.

'Like a golden syrup sandwich,' she sighed. 'But of gold!' She pulled at a jag of rock, trying to prise open a crack so that she could take some of that grey stone with the streak of gold through it to show Fa. But . . .

Grrrrrooar!

A great rumbling growl made the back of Ida's head prickle with fear. She looked up. There, silhouetted against a darkly threatening sky, was the bear, mouth open to show terrible teeth and to sound out a terrible roar. Then a great golden flash of light tore raggedly through the dark sky behind the bear, and a great grumble of angry thunder shook the sky and earth as heavy rain began to fall.

I only wanted to take enough to show Fa what he has worked so hard for, thought Ida! Doesn't he deserve that? And she rose, as furious as the bear, and roared back at it!

She raised her fists full of nuggets and ran at that Klondike bear, just as lightning flashed yellow again in the dark sky, crashing so powerfully to earth that Ida felt it thud in her chest, and the thunder joined her own roaring. Whether it was Ida or the storm that frightened the bear, Ida couldn't tell, but the bear swiftly twisted its big body and fled, crashing through bushes, and away.

Ida ran the other way now, down, down towards the valley, as rain soaked the land and also soaked her. Her gold-filled pockets thumped clumsily, bruisingly, against her legs. Ida ran from the beautiful wilderness of reds and oranges and gold and darkness and the bear, and towards mess and litter and people. Back to Fa with her gold.

29

Back at Little Eldorado, Ida tried to shout out, but she had little breath left.

'Fa,' she panted faintly. 'Fa?'

'There you are!'

Fa had come back to life since this morning. He stood up straight and there was colour in his skin. 'I have been wondering where in the world you had got to!' He held out his arms to Ida, hugging her tight as she got to him and as she panted against his chest.

'Fa, I've . . .' began Ida, but Fa wasn't listening.

'Such exciting news, Ida . . . Carrie is having her baby!'

'Now?'

'Yes. And, would you believe, I played a small part in helping her.' Fa shrugged as if to suggest that what he had done was something small, but Ida could see that he was pleased with himself.

'You see, I was out looking to see where you had gone.' Fa was steering Ida back to their cabin now. 'I thought that you must be in the berry patch. You weren't there, but Carrie was. I found her bent double with pains, quite unable to make her way home and too far from the mines for her calls for help to be heard. So I carried her home.'

'But she's so big and heavy!' said Ida in astonishment as she pictured skinny Fa with stocky Carrie and her big baby bump.

'She is indeed!' laughed Fa. 'But I had the strength to do it. Carried her home and put her to bed, then summoned Nathan and went for Mrs Olsen down the valley. She's the one who knows about babies. So they are all in there,' Fa waved towards the McKenzie cabin. 'And there should be a small new life in this valley very shortly. Oh, it reminds me so of when you were born, my love.' Fa laughed an easy laugh that made Ida join in. 'Such a very special time! Gracious, look at the state of you! Come out of the rain and let's get you dry!'

Ida set the kettle on the stove to make tea while Fa changed out of his own wet clothes. The pouring rain outside made a soft kind of noise all around and it was nice to be cosy together in their little home, thinking of Carrie and Nathan and, soon, a baby in the little home across the way.

Something stopped Ida from capping Fa's story with her own tale of finding gold. As she took off her wet skirt, she carefully folded the pockets, heavy and lumpy with the golden nuggets, so that they stayed hidden for the moment. This is Fa's moment, not mine, she thought. Fa had a new kind of energy. He made Ida sit, wrapped her in a blanket, and made her tea. He's pleased with himself, thought Ida. That's good.

'Today has been a strange one,' said Fa, pouring tea into enamelled mugs. 'It has reminded me that life itself is real riches. We have the gift of life, Ida, and must value that.' Fa sipped his steaming tin cup of tea. Then he winked at Ida. 'Guess what? I have a new plan.'

'Fa!' Ida jumped up, spilling her tea. 'No, Fa!'

Fa laughed. 'A simple plan that really will work.' He looked Ida in the eye. 'It is time that you and I went home, my dear.'

But I've just found gold, thought Ida!

Fa pushed a hand through his tangled wet hair, shook his head and laughed. 'Have I been somewhat mad these last weeks?' Ida nodded. Perhaps you still are a little mad, she thought. You have forgotten something important.

'How can we give up looking for gold when we have to find gold before we can go home? We need quite a lot of money for train and boat tickets, remember.' Shall I tell him about the gold? But Fa was smiling.

'Didn't I always promise you that I would keep back the money for our return trip?'

'Yes, but you didn't keep any back!' said Ida. 'Or at least, if you did, it has gone now. Spent or stolen or something. I looked everywhere for it when you were ill and I'm sorry Fa but it is gone.' She was about to tell him that the loss of the money didn't matter because she had now found gold, but . . .

'Aha!' Fa patted underneath his armpits and gave a

naughty kind of grin. 'You aren't the only seamstress around here!' Fa opened up his tweed jacket to reveal . . .

'There's nothing there,' said Ida. 'I already looked.'

'But there is something,' said Fa. 'Bank notes hidden inside the lining.' Fa, patted the jacket. 'Stitched safe within, where no pickpocket could reach because they aren't in a pocket.'

'Oh! So that's why . . .'

'I wouldn't let you wash my jacket,' said Fa. He looked earnestly at Ida. 'You know, Ida, I never did lose sight of the important fact that I must take you safely home again, however irresponsible I may have been in other ways.' Fa shrugged. 'Goodness, if I hadn't had you with me, then maybe I really would have risked everything for gold.

'But you did risk your own health!' said Ida. 'You were most terribly ill, you know, and you said that there was no money for a doctor.'

'Because there wasn't,' said Fa. 'I knew that I must keep enough of Grandmama's money to take you home.' Fa shrugged. 'Mind you, I haven't been so very clever now that I come to think of it. This money will buy our tickets, but it won't pay for food and new clothes or any of our other needs as we travel. And I had so hoped to make enough to set us up in a new life once we arrived back in England, and at the very least to arrive home looking respectable.'

'Aha!' said Ida. 'Well you don't have to worry about that. We will have quite enough money because . . .'

'. . . because you have been earning with your wonderful pies and helping Carrie with washing. You are a wonder, Ida. And if I work as we go, maybe taking a position on board the boat or somesuch, then I think it might just be enough.'

So Ida said nothing about the gold she had found.

Fa is happy because he was able to rescue Carrie and because he has the money for tickets home. If I tell him about the gold, will he want to stay in the Klondike after all? Would another winter make him ill again, perhaps even kill him? Or would it let him go home in triumph? Ida couldn't decide.

So, for the moment, she said nothing.

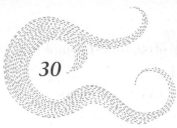

30

Ida hardly slept that night, her mind awhirl with thoughts. Outside the rain stormed, lightning flashed and thunder rumbled.

Ida thought of England. She thought of the gentle seasons there and of her friends. Of Mama's grave in the church by the big house. Of Grandmama and all of them in Yewdale Hall. She thought of milk puddings and stews with dumplings bobbing on the top, of freshly-dug potatoes, freshly-picked tomatoes, freshly-laid eggs. She thought of her gold find. Of how, if Fa did get excited by news of it, they might stay in the Klondike after all and not go home. How do I feel about that, she asked herself, and she had no answer.

She thought of Grandmama scoffing that Fa would never succeed in the Klondike and how pleasing it might be to prove her wrong, even if that did mean more long long months of darkness as they stayed another long hard winter of waiting until they could harvest the gold. Another winter away from Norfolk, Minnie and visiting Mama's grave. What would make Fa truly happy? If Ida helped him to triumph, she would have justified her coming with him in the most pleasing way. But there were such dangers in staying! Round and round the possibilities churned in Ida's mind.

Ida was still awake as the storm slid away. Outside, the cabin settled to quietness and dawn lightened the cold sky. Then there came a sudden shout.

'Metcalf? Ida?'

'That's Nathan. Oh, it must be Carrie's baby!' said Ida. She jumped up from her mattress and pushed aside the blanket hanging in the doorway. There was a pink-faced Nathan, joyfully jumping over piles of muddy diggings, then dancing a jig in the pink early morning light.

'He's born! We have a son!'

'How lovely!' said Ida. 'Can I see him, please? I have never seen a really new baby. And I want to see Carrie too, of course.'

'Sure you can!' smiled Nathan. 'Mrs Olsen sent me out whilst she freshened up Carrie, and I thought to myself that the two of you Metcalfs just might be eager to hear the news. Besides, I was just about bursting-full to tell somebody!'

'That's marvellous, McKenzie!' said Fa, striding out to greet Nathan with outstretched hand. 'Very many congratulations!'

Ida dressed as quickly as she could, pulling on petticoats, skirt and blouse, stockings and boots and a shawl. Her hand touched the heavy weight of gold nuggets in the damp skirt pockets and she quickly emptied them onto her bed, hiding the nuggets under her pillow.

'Come on, Fa!'

'I really don't think that it is suitable for a man to burst in on a lady who has so recently given birth, you know,' said Fa, striding through the mud. 'You just give Carrie my congratulations, Ida, and I will wait outside with Nathan.'

As they got near to the McKenzie cabin, Ida could hear sounds from inside: murmuring women's voices and a sharp small call that sounded as if it might be from a wild animal. The baby! She suddenly felt shy of the new little person in the McKenzies' lives. Perhaps Fa was right and it was intruding to push into this little family that wasn't even related in any way to them. But, 'Ida?' called Carrie from inside. 'That you? Come right in and meet my boy!'

Carrie was sitting in a crumpled bed, her newly brushed hair loose around her shining, smiling face. And somebody very small indeed, wrapped in sheeting, lay in her scooped arm.

'Well, what do you think?' asked Carrie, pushing back the wrapping from the baby's face. Ida stepped closer. The baby's face was crumpled and red and cross-looking. Ida laughed and Carrie did too. 'He looks more like my mother-in-law than I care for!' she said. 'But he'll soon baby-out and lose that. Do you want a hold of him?'

'Oh, can I?' Ida bent her own arms and took the baby into them. He was surprisingly heavy and solid. 'Do you feel light without him inside you?' she asked, then she blushed because perhaps she shouldn't be thinking about where the baby had come from and how it had got out. But Carrie just laughed again.

'Don't rightly know how I feel, except kind of amazed that this small person came from inside of me. And I'm hungry. I know that for sure!'

'Oh, I can help with that,' said Ida. 'I'll cook you something good.'

Ida was allowed to step outside with the baby to show him to Fa. Fa held out a finger to touch the damp, spiky black hair on the baby's head, then he shook his own head and smiled.

'What a miracle new life is every time,' he said.

It was a lovely and a strange day, cooking with Fa in a gentle and unhurried way. Every so often, as she rolled out pastry with a glass bottle, Ida thought of that rich seam of gold in the mountains. Yesterday seemed distant now, perhaps not even real. Fa was happy, plucking a fine fat goose that Mr Mulroony had shot as it flew southwards overhead.

'Something for a celebration, to welcome the new baby,' he had said when he brought it to their door. 'Nathan said to deliver it to you for cooking.' Mr Mulroony wouldn't take any payment for the goose. In fact he left a shiny dollar, with instructions that the coin was to be given to the McKenzies for their baby. 'Place that in his little palm for good fortune,' he said. 'That's what we do back home and no reason we shouldn't do it here just as well.' People are nice, thought Ida. Everything felt so peaceful and right, somehow. The gold can wait, Ida decided.

Fa made stuffing for the goose from wild onion and breadcrumbs and chopped dandelion leaves. Ida cooked their last reconstituted potato and peas. And she made a good thick gravy from the meat juices, adding flour.

'That smells exceptionally good,' said Fa, as he lifted the bird from the oven.

'It's not for us, remember,' said Ida. 'It's for the McKenzies.' But, of course, Nathan and Carrie insisted that they all share the meal together.

'And one day I shall tell this baby here of the fine goose dinner cooked by our friends Ida and Frank Metcalf,' said Carrie.

'And we can tell him that he missed out on eating his share by being just too darn young,' smiled Nathan.

'You know, I was so wishing my own folk could be here to see this little one,' said Carrie, sitting up in bed with a plate full of steaming food on her lap. But this feels like family to me. Wouldn't you say so, Little Sister Ida?'

'I do, Big Sister Carrie!' laughed Ida, but then she looked across at Fa, and she saw him clear his throat. She suddenly knew what he was going to tell Carrie and Nathan.

'You know,' said Fa. 'Ida and I enormously value your friendship and the kindness you have shown us in our time here. But . . .' Ida held her breath.

'. . . You're going to leave,' said Carrie, her knife and

223

fork resting on her plate as if her appetite had suddenly gone. 'I knew it.' Ida looked at Fa.

'We are indeed going to leave,' agreed Fa. 'I have been a fool in thinking that I could make a living for us in finding gold. I haven't done so and I don't see myself as a farmer, capable of making a living from the rough land here. Besides,' Fa looked at Ida. 'I must take Ida back to her Mama's family. She needs schooling and a different kind of life if she is to fulfil the life her mother would have wanted for her. I must earn a proper living and make a proper home for her.'

Carrie sighed. 'We surely will miss the both of you.' Then she looked at Nathan. 'Should we tell them?'

'As good a time as any,' said Nathan. He stood up and cleared his throat and put his hands behind his back. 'Mr Frank Metcalf, Sir, my Carrie and me, we have decided upon something. After what you did yesterday, finding and helping my Carrie . . .'

'Oh, that wasn't anything!' said Fa, his neck blushing pink, then stopping because Nathan gave him a look.

'After what you did, we would like to name our son after the man who was there when help was needed. Mr Metcalf . . .'

'Frank, please.'

'Frank. We hope to call our son after you. He will be Frank Metcalf McKenzie, but only if you're agreeable to that, of course.'

Ida beamed. 'Oh, that's a splendid name!'

'Ain't it just?' smiled Carrie, and she began eating her goose once more.

And Fa sat there, red-faced with embarrassment, with tears shining on his cheeks, a huge smile on his face, and his hands clasped together.

And I can make him happier still, thought Ida, and she knew that she would tell him about the gold after all, but not in front of the McKenzies.

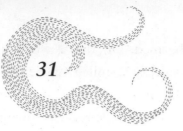

31

They carried the empty pots and plates back to Little Eldorado.

'This is one day when I am happy to wash dishes,' said Fa, hitching the basket up his bony arm. 'Nobody should be washing dishes in a house where a new baby has just been born. That's a moment when life should just pause in wonder.'

It wasn't until they were washing the pots together, Fa washing and Ida drying, that Ida finally asked, 'Fa, how would you feel if you made a big gold find now?'

'Well, that's about as likely as your Grandmama joining the morris men and dancing with bells around her ankles and a stick in her hand!' laughed Fa.

'But, just supposing . . . ? Would it be nice?'

'It would be marvellous, of course,' said Fa. 'But I really don't mind that it won't happen, you know. So you mustn't worry about that.'

'But it will!' Ida flapped at Fa with her drying cloth. 'The thing is, it has already happened!'

'I beg your pardon?' said Fa, hands dripping.

'Truly!' laughed Ida. 'I have found gold! Lots of it! All we have to do is go and get it.'

'Good gracious!' said Fa. He threw the washcloth into the bowl with the dirty pots, wiped his hands on his trousers, and pulled Ida over to sit by the stove. 'You'd better explain exactly what this is all about.'

Ida took a deep breath. The birth of little Frank had postponed this moment, but now the excitement of her news was bubbling up inside her again. She was giving Fa the gift of a dream come true!

'Well,' she said. 'You remember when I was cross yesterday morning and I ran off?' Fa nodded. 'Well, I went up into the mountains, further than I've been before, and . . . um . . .' Ida made an apologetic kind of face at Fa, and shrugged. 'I got chased by a bear.'

'You got cha– Good gracious, Ida! A bear? Are you sure?' Fa was off his seat and pacing, arms waving, then laughing because he realised that of course you would be sure if you had been chased by a bear. 'You got chased by a bear and you didn't feel that was worth mentioning to me a little sooner than this?'

'But Carrie's baby was being born and . . .'

'Oh, of course, of course! Gracious, my dear, dear girl!' Fa flung his long arms around her, holding her secure. 'However did you get away from the bear? Glory, I'm so very glad that you did! But, what happened? Was it a large bear?'

So Ida told him about the bear that was very big indeed but which didn't chase, and how she still ran from it and tripped. And how that had landed her on top of a tumble of golden nuggets, with more gold in the rock beneath.

Ida reached under the covers on her bed and produced a handful of golden nuggets. 'Look. And there is so much more.' She tipped her hand one way and then another, making the gold wink in the firelight. Fa touched the soft nuggets with a finger.

'Beautiful,' he said.

'Hold them!' Ida tipped them into Fa's big hands. 'There is so much, much more that we can take. Really, truly a fortune this time, Fa! Enough to impress Grandmama, even. We can pick up the nuggets and then there is more that we can hack out of the rock. But we will have to be a bit secret about it, don't you think? Otherwise every miner around here will go racing there, wanting it for a claim.' She looked at Fa. 'I think that we should mark out our own claim in sticks, then hurry to get it registered in Dawson. We will have to sell this claim first, of course, since you aren't allowed more than one claim and I'm not allowed any claim because I'm not old enough. Fa?'

Fa was strangely quiet, gazing at the nuggets in his hands. Ida thumped him on the arm, wanting a reaction. 'We should make a claim straight away, don't you think? We can get lots of gold because we can use some of it to buy proper machinery to dig out the gold, just as Big Dennis did. Maybe we could even buy explosives to blast the stone and gold out of the ground. That's what people are using in some places, Carrie says. Oh, stop laughing, Fa!'

Fa was chuckling now. He had put the nuggets onto the table. His arms were folded and he was stroking his beard and looking down at Ida with twinkling eyes. 'You are throwing your arms around, Miss Metcalf!'

'What has that to do with . . . ?'

'Remember how you told me once that I always wave my arms around when I'm explaining a really poor sort of an idea? Well, I think this idea of yours is a poor one.'

'But it's what you so wanted! You can be rich. We can buy a house in Norfolk and you won't need to work and . . .'

Fa took Ida into his arms and hugged her tight, even as she thrashed to escape. 'No,' said Fa. 'No, no, no, no, my dear. If we sell our claim and register another the whole of Dawson will soon be abuzz with rumours and a mass of desperate men will be stalking after us to see where we go, ready to stake claims themselves in any place that looks likely to offer gold. We might mine some gold . . .'

'Lots of it!' protested Ida. 'It just needs hacking out of . . .'

'Hacking,' said Fa. 'You tell me that this place is beautiful. Do you really want to see it "hacked"? And exploded? And spoiled as this valley has been?'

Ida thought of those beautiful autumn trees and the birds. The quiet. And the bear who hadn't chased her. 'No,' she said slowly. 'But . . .'

'Do you really want to spend months and months of frozen dark winter here?' Fa let Ida wriggle free.

'I thought that you would be pleased!' Ida scowled. 'I thought that you would be happy at last.'

'But I am happy,' said Fa. 'Truly! There is a part of me that feels a nice little lift of triumph that a Metcalf has found some of the gold that the Klondike had been keeping so successfully hidden. That is pleasing.' He shrugged. 'But I find, rather to my surprise, that I don't want to fight the country for its riches any more, even if we could win this time. Besides, we haven't the time to go mining a new place if we are to leave before the freeze this year. I have neither the energy nor the inclination for another Canadian winter, Ida. That particular madness is over.' Ida looked at Fa's tired face and realised that was true. Fa took one of her hands in his. 'I do think that it really is time to go home.'

'Can I at least show you the place?' said Ida. 'So that you can see it for yourself?'

'I would like that,' said Fa, and he patted Ida's hand. 'I would like that very much indeed.'

32

Next day, Ida took Fa's hand and led him along the valley and up into the mountains, above and away from the mining, and into a land of fantastically coloured trees. To her surprise, Ida found that she could remember the way, although she worried that she might not be able to find the gold once they got into the mountains. They walked and walked, clambering over fallen trees, wading through bog, pushing through thorn bushes, up to the clearer high place where Ida had been before. As they walked, Ida jumped to snatch some red and orange and green leaves from trees.

'To take home, so that you can remember the colours for painting,' she said.

Fa said little, but whenever they stopped for a rest, he stood tall and looked all around. 'Beautiful,' he said each time. 'Truly truly beautiful.' And one of the times that he said that, he was looking at Ida.

Ida found the slope of mountainside she remembered. 'There were trees in a line, and the special tree with orange leaves standing just over the place where the gold was.' She frowned. 'That looks like the trees, except that I can't see the special one.'

'Never mind,' said Fa. 'I am glad to have seen this wonderful place, gold or no gold.'

'Oh, but . . . !' Ida grabbed Fa's arm and pointed. There, on the ground in the middle of the row of trees, lay the charred remains of a large tree.' Ida felt a little sick.

'Struck by lightning,' said Fa.

That storm. The fury of the bear, of the place, of Ida herself, all came rushing back to her. Ida felt as if she was trespassing on land that wasn't meant for people.

Fa squeezed Ida's hand. 'So, you played with bears and with lightning, did you? Quite an adventure!'

Ida let go of Fa's hand and ran to the blackened tree stump. She bent down and pushed aside the burnt branches that had tumbled onto the charred grass.

'Pull up the roots and soil around here, Fa. You'll find . . .'

'Gracious, look at this!' said Fa, holding up a sooty but glinting lump between large finger and thumb. 'My first nugget!'

'I told you!' said Ida. She laughed because the nugget Fa had found was as big as a hazelnut; bigger than any she had found.

'Must be worth, what, possibly twenty dollars?' said Fa. 'They do say you find the larger lumps of gold high up and finer stuff the further you go along the river system – the heaviest being dropped by the river first, of course. But up here? Miles from any stream?'

'A stream must have been here thousands of years ago,' said Ida. 'Maybe before there were people, even. Even before bears.'

'Amazing.' Fa scratched his head. 'Perhaps there is still a stream underground? That would explain why the trees grow in a line.'

They both scrabbled around in the singed earth and, over the next hour or so, they found seven more gold nuggets.

'You look a regular sweep's boy,' smiled Fa. 'I dare say that I do too.' He brushed soil off his hands and looked across to the setting sun. 'The sun is on its way down and I think that we should do the same.'

'Can we just try and take a bit of the stone with gold inside it?' said Ida. Fa bent and traced the line of gold in the stone. He took out his penknife and worked it into a crevice in the stone, levering to detach a small sharp shard of the crystalline rock with gold streaking through it. Then he looked up at Ida. 'That is enough to be a memento.' Ida smiled, relieved somehow that the task felt completed.

Fa stood up, jiggling the nuggets in his big palm. 'We have quite enough to pay for all we need and why take more than that? Her Majesty, Queen Victoria, owns a whole Empire and any number of jewels and any amount of money, but is she happier than we are just now, do you suppose?' Fa shook his head. 'Sufficient is all that's needed for happiness.'

They began to walk back downhill. The air was fresh. Birds sang.

'Your Mama was a wise one, Ida. She knew about enough being enough. Your Grandmama couldn't understand how her daughter could settle for so much less than she had been brought up to. I don't think that I quite dared to believe it myself when Mama insisted that she really was happy with just me and you and our small home. But I do believe that now. That is a consoling thought.'

They talked of Mama as they walked back down to the valley. They talked of going home and of what they would leave behind, here in the Klondike.

'Would you like me to have a word with Nathan?' asked Fa. 'I could tell him where that gold of yours is to be found. He might like to go and find it after we are gone. I do think that he will have a more sensible idea of how to handle such a find than I do. He and Carrie may need a better income if they are going to care well for that baby of theirs.'

'Little Frank,' smiled Ida.

They walked on in silence for a while, then Ida said, 'The Klondike likes us for not taking all that we could have, don't you think?'

'I was thinking much the same thing myself,' said Fa. The sinking sun shone through coloured, waving leaves, glinting in a chill evening breeze.

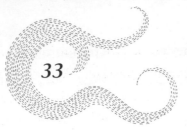

33

They left the valley in the last week of September. Snow covered the scarred landscape, making it strangely beautiful in a way that they had never seen it before.

'Bears'll be hibernating now the geese are flying south,' said Carrie. She had little Frank wrapped warmly and slung against her in a shawl, Indian style. 'I guess you're doing the same as those geese.'

'Except that Ida's one of them fairy tale kinds of a goose,' said Nathan. 'She's gone and laid a golden egg right here on our doorstep.' He winked at Ida.

'Nice to know it's there,' said Carrie. 'Nice too to have the winter to contemplate how best to handle the find so's we're not rushing in and doing it all wrong.'

'I'll write letters to you,' promised Ida. That was all she could manage to say before tears came. But she hugged Carrie and pushed Duffle into her arms. 'For little Frank,' she said.

Nathan shook Fa's hand. 'A great honour to know you and your charming family,' said Fa.

They hefted their packs onto their backs, and set off for Dawson. The gold was heavy in their packs and heavy in their minds too. But the rest of their luggage was simply what they needed for the journey – some food, some clothes, a cup and blanket each. As well as those red, orange and yellow leaves packed between clean cloths and pressed between the pages of Fa's Bible, plus one eagle feather and two stones with holes through them.

'It feels wrong, leaving so many big things behind,' said Ida. 'It took three weeks of laundry work before I could buy the big pan.'

'Life changes and our needs have changed,' said Fa. 'Carrie will be glad of the extra pans, I'm sure. Besides, don't you find your pack heavy enough as it is?' Ida did. The constant weight on her back brought back memories of the weeks spent on the Chilkoot Pass. It would be good to head south before winter got a grip this year.

They didn't talk much on the days spent walking back to Dawson. They paid a few cents to sleep on floors and to eat food from other miners' claim shanties. Fa was still not fully well or strong. The weather was cold and getting colder. They passed many abandoned claims with tools and rubbish lying around. There were a few graves with poor wooden crosses amongst the debris.

The walking took most of their energy, but there was the Klondike to observe and to remember, and lots to think about. The nearer they got to Dawson, the more the land had been spoiled and the more people there were. Ida felt excited, but also strangely sad.

Dawson had changed in the months since Ida had last

seen it. Freshly built timber buildings had replaced many of the tents. There was a boardwalk to lift people up off the mud in the streets. There were more saloons, more hotels and shops and laundries and lemonade bars and bakeries and barbers and dentists and just about everything. There was even a railway being built to take people over the White Pass and down the Yukon.

'It's a different world, and all in a matter of weeks,' said Fa.

'There are more women than before,' said Ida, noting some girls in bright skirts and with rouged faces of a kind which Grandmama would certainly not have approved. Those girls giggled together and Ida suddenly missed the giggling groups of girls she had been a part of back in the village school. She missed Minnie.

'Those are show girls,' said Fa. 'Making a deal of money off men who like to look at a pretty girl singing or dancing in a theatre.'

'Perhaps I could have made us more money if . . .'

'No you certainly could not!' said Fa. 'Gracious! It really is high time I got you safe home to England!

'Can I please write to Grandmama tonight? There is so much to tell,' said Ida.

'I doubt it is worth sending anything now,' said Fa. 'Any letter that you post will more or less travel with us. It won't get to England any faster than we do ourselves, and then of course you can tell her all you want in person.' Fa tugged at his beard. 'But, thinking of letters, I suppose there is just a chance that somebody may have written a letter to us since we've been gone. We might ask in the mail office if they have anything under our name.'

And they did.

The Dower House
Yewdale Hall
Cheshire

27 August 1898

My dear Frank and Ida,

'Goodness!' said Fa. 'That's the first time your Grandmama has ever addressed me as "dear".'

'Shush, I'm reading,' said Ida.

You may thank your acquaintance, Mr Selwyn Stanley, if this letter ever reaches you.

'Stanley? Good God!'

'Shush!'

It was Mr Stanley who told me that it was possible to write to the post office in a place called Dawson, and that it is the custom for those living in the wilds to collect post from that office. Fortunately for me, the post has worked remarkably well, if a little slowly, in the other direction. Ida, my dear, I do thank you for your news, and particularly for the descriptions of the places through which you have travelled.

I have your letters kept safe in my bureau, tied with a ribbon: there to be re-read if ever I want some amusement, or to feel close to you, or to wonder yet again at what you are doing. Do you know, when I read your letters I really feel as though I am there myself, climbing that dreadfully steep chilly mountain place that you wrote of and carrying such burdens.

'Huh! Can you imagine . . . ?'
'Shush, Fa!'

As you know, those adventures aren't quite what I had in mind for Isabella's daughter and I was far from pleased to learn that you had absconded abroad and away from education, but I do admire what you and your father have done, nevertheless.

'Really?'

Your father is an uncommon man; unusually determined to see things through once he has decided upon a thing. That is admirable. And I so admire your own spirit and bravery, Ida, and your excellent judgment of people. You inherit that from your mother, who inherited it from me, of course. Which brings me back to Mr Stanley.

Ida, my dear, if you had not sent that letter recording the dreadful way in which that man had treated your father and yourself, well, I have to confess that I might very well have fallen for his stories just as readily as your father did. Your tale of woe acted as a warning, arriving in the morning post the very day that Mr Stanley turned up at Yewdale Hall, asking for favours on the strength of his supposed great friendship with my son-in-law and granddaughter. A clever plan, you must agree, since he clearly knew all about you and would have convinced me entirely of his friendship with you had it not been for the words I had read from you that morning. He even gave me articles which I would know had come from you (I have that rather ordinary little brooch that your mother liked to wear, Ida) which he claimed were sent by you as 'proof' of your association.

'Mama's brooch is safe!'

Fa clasped Ida's hand as they read on together.

Mr Stanley had the effrontery to tell me that you,

Frank, had made a promise that I would be happy to lend him some money. He told me that you would be bringing home gold to more than that value very shortly and would repay me for his loan. He told me that you owed the money to him.

Well, I knew otherwise, of course! I knew that he, Mr Stanley, was nothing better than a common thief, for all that he claims to be of old family stock. Worse than a thief! A swindler too! With no excuse at all, because I believe his family truly is of good standing. But he has gone to the bad. It made me think, Frank, that upbringing and background is not everything when it comes to the making of a gentleman.

I think that it might amuse you to know that I played along with Mr Stanley's ploy for a while, intrigued to see quite how he would play his little game out. But the moment came when I could not resist a tease.

'I believe you served in the cavalry with my son, Stephen?' I said. Well, Mr Stanley turned pale.

'How do you come to know that, Lady Berringer?' he asked.

'Never mind how,' I told him. 'But how fortunate for you that my son is here today. I just heard his steps coming up the stairs.' And in walked Stephen, splendid in his uniform, sword at his side. (He had been to have his portrait painted for the dining hall.)

Well! You can imagine the scene that unfolded. Stephen restrained Stanley as the wretch attempted to escape and Mr Stanley is currently in jail and awaiting trial. I shall offer your letter as evidence in court, Ida my dear.

Now, to the more important part of my letter. Mr Stanley told lies, so I do not suppose for a moment that you have found great quantities of gold as he told me you had. I am not the stupid woman that he supposed me to be. I do read the papers and have read tales of a few fortunes made, but many more fortunes lost. Let me simply make clear, my dear Frank, that I very much hope that you will bring Ida home as soon as possible, fortune or no fortune; I care not. I admire what you have achieved together with your daughter. Indeed, I find myself even a little envious of your adventures. You shall return rich in stories, if nothing more, and I am impatient to welcome you both and to hear more. Please do not submit yourselves to another of those dreadful winters. My hope is that there was one truth in what Mr Stanley told us: that you will be home shortly.

This letter may or may not reach you, of course. But if you are reading it, then it clearly has done so. The garden here at the Dower House is glorious with late, sweet-smelling sweet peas, and a mass of fresh fruit and vegetables. Your Aunt Helen is doing

unspeakable things to the décor of the big house.
Tilly is married and we all miss her. Your cousin Eric
has done something too disgraceful for me to set
down in writing. I myself am well at the moment,
although my bunions trouble me, and who can tell
how long my health may last?

But, at present, I remain your loving mother-in-
law and Grandmama,

Adelaide Berringer

'Well!' said Fa.

'She is nice really,' said Ida. 'Otherwise how could Mama, who was so very nice, have come from her?'

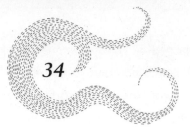

34

They sold Little Eldorado at an agency in Dawson for considerably less than they had paid for it. Then they celebrated the sale with a drink of pink lemonade and a proper meal, with napkins on laps and flowers on the table, in a hotel.

'The price I got for the claim was about the price of those two tins of condensed milk I bought when we first arrived,' said Fa. 'But the truth is, we have been lucky to sell it at all with so many leaving the Klondike. Besides, Little Eldorado never yielded much.'

'I hope that whoever moves in there will be good friends for Carrie and Nathan,' said Ida. It was such a relief not to care very much about money now that they had enough of it. They had taken their heavy gold to the bank, where it had been weighed, and now they had a fat pile of dollar bills that were so much lighter to carry. Ida wasn't sure which felt of greater value – lumps of metal or printed pieces of paper.

'You can't eat or wear either sort of wealth,' she said. 'I suppose that is why animals and birds do not bother with money of any kind.'

'Humankind is strange indeed,' said Fa. 'But rather wonderful, all the same.'

Fa used the worn old bills from his jacket to pay for their tickets, just as he had always planned. They boarded a paddle steamer that would take them from Dawson, down the Yukon River, out to sea, and then south around the coast to Skagway. They stood at the ship's railings as the paddles thrashed the waters, and the sights and smells and sounds of Dawson shrank away from them.

'This time last year . . .' said Fa, and he didn't need to say anything else. The two of them stood and looked and remembered all that had happened. Dawson shrank small and the mountains behind seemed to loom larger as they eased down the river and looked back.

'You should paint this,' said Ida.

'I was just thinking about painting,' said Fa. 'Except that I was thinking about a possible picture of your golden place. Those marvellous red and yellow and orange leaves, the greens and browns and black and white, and some blue in the sky. That black broken tree.'

'And a tiny glint of gold that only you and I will know is there,' said Ida.

'It would be good to be creating things again,' said Fa. 'Making things, instead of taking either Berringer money from your Grandmama or gold from a beautiful land. I must find a way to make a living.'

'But we did make things,' said Ida. 'We made friends! And no end of meals and beds and tools and pies and pie dishes and, oh, all sorts.'

'All of that was achieved much more by you than me,' said Fa. 'I was so busy digging. And all for nothing.' Fa shook his head. 'Time for a new start, I think.'

They boarded the Rosalie in Skagway, steaming further down the coast and then inland again to Vancouver.

'The twenty-second of October,' said Fa, looking at his first up-to-date newspaper for a very long time. 'How do you feel about Christmas at home?' Ida wondered if he meant the big house or Norfolk, or somewhere else entirely.

Fa clapped his hands together. 'Now that we have money we must buy new clothes to make ourselves respectable for society once again. We could perhaps do a little Christmas shopping as well.'

So, in Vancouver, the two of them went down the shopping streets, enjoying being able to linger and take their time.

'The race is over. Oh, isn't that a relief!' said Fa.

Fa had his hair and beard trimmed at a barbers' shop. They bought Ida a new skirt, and blouses and a jacket, and a new warm coat because her wrists were sticking out of the worn blue one. New lace-up ladies' boots too. And moleskin trousers and three new shirts for Fa.

'I've no need for a new jacket,' said Fa. 'This one has served me well, and it will continue to serve me well. Besides, I am fond of it.' Fa stroked his trim short beard in the mirror and grinned. 'This finery is all very well and good,' he said. 'But we can afford to buy some less necessary items too. Presents and whatnot.'

They bought Fa an Indian moose hide jacket, with tassels that were decorated with porcupine quills and beadwork all around the neck. 'I can wear it to dinner when your Uncle Stephen is in his dress uniform!' said Fa.

Ida thumped him. 'Don't you dare! Grandmama would have a fainting fit and need her salts if she saw you in that!' said Ida.

'Then we must find something to turn Grandmama native too,' said Fa. So they bought Grandmama some beautiful moccasins, also decorated with coloured beads.

'They will be soft for her bunions,' said Ida. 'I would like to get something for Tilly as well. A wedding present. And I suppose we should take gifts back for the cousins and aunts.'

'And I have thought of something important that I want to arrange and buy for you,' said Fa.

'What is it?'

'Wait and see.'

Fa led Ida to a jeweller's shop where gold was worked into all sorts of ornaments for prospectors to take home to wives and mothers and daughters.

'Can I be of assistance?' asked the jeweller, taking a spyglass from his eye and coming to the counter. Fa took a handkerchief from his pocket, and unwrapped it to reveal the small shard of crystalline rock streaked with gold that he had taken from the golden place. He put the rock onto the counter.

'Would it be possible to work some kind of a ring to display this stone? It would be for my daughter here.'

'Why, certainly,' said the jeweller. 'I have rings of that description already made up, if you are wanting to take something right now.'

Fa shook his head. 'No, I think that we want a ring to carry this very particular piece of rock, don't we, Ida? We can delay travel for a day or two.'

35

On the train across Canada, and then on the ship crossing the choppy seas of the Atlantic Ocean back to England, Ida often gazed at that ring on her finger, at the smoothly polished oval slice of Klondike where dark and grey rock carried within it a solid splash of warm rich gold.

Fa was growing strong and well again, resting, eating well and enjoying chats with fellow passengers on the voyage. One evening he came to where Ida was leaning on the rails of the ship, watching the sea. Fa's hands were waving, and his eyes were twinkling. 'I have found what I was after.'

'It was me who found the gold, remember,' said Ida.

'I don't mean gold,' said Fa. 'What I have found is what I want to do with my life now.'

'Tell me,' said Ida.

'I shall enter the church – become a vicar.'

'Truly?' said Ida. She looked up at Fa. 'Isn't that what Grandmama suggested a long time ago, and you said you would not?'

'Ha!' laughed Fa, arms waving. 'She did, and I scorned the idea.'

'You'd be a nice vicar,' said Ida.

'Thank you, my dear. I do think that maybe I could help people to see something of the wonders of God's world. And maybe, more to the point, help them through their hard times. Gracious, to think that the old trout might have been right all along!'

'Fa!'

Fa smiled. 'I am a little like the Yukon River that starts its journey just fifteen miles from the Pacific Ocean, then wanders for more than two thousand miles before it gets to that same sea. We're going back very much to where we began. But, oh, I feel differently.'

'Will we be able to live in a vicarage in Norfolk?' asked Ida. 'Near to Minnie and Jim and all the others?'

Fa ruffled her hair. 'Very possibly, my dear wise daughter. Very possibly. I will certainly need you for my "pardner", at least for a while longer.' Fa pulled his battered notebook from a jacket pocket and leafed through early pages until he found what he wanted. 'Here,' he said. 'I noted this down from the book that the doctor on the train showed us all those months ago.'

Fa read from the page: '"Men may be chums in easy, prosperous times, but it is not until they pass together through a succession of dangers and hardships that they can become pardners. Pardners stand as one under all vicissitudes, doubling each other's joy and dividing sorrows and failures." Well, my dear Ida, you have certainly done that for me.'

Ida thumped him on the arm, and that arm pulled her into a hug against the dirty old tweed jacket, and she thought how very pleased Mama would be with how it had all turned out.

Legend has that if the ravens leave the Tower of London, then monarch and kingdom will fall.

London, 1666. The Great Plague rages and the city is a dangerous place. Young Nick Truelove blames King Charles II for the hardships he faces and vows revenge.

Inspired by the wily cunning of a raven, he bluff his way into the centre of the King's power - the Tower of London. But as a remarkable friendship grows between boy and raven, a new danger engulfs London. Nick's view of his world and his King is about to change forever.

WARS THAT SEEMED A WORLD AWAY WERE BROUGHT TO THEIR DOORSTEPS . . . AND INTO THEIR HEARTS

TROUBLE ON CABLE STREET

JOAN LINGARD

London, 1936.

Riots are brewing in the East End as a country broken by one war lives in fear of another.

With one brother run away to fight for revolution in Spain and the other lured in by the Fascists, Isabella is faced with a conflict of her own.

As she battles to keep her family together, Isabella wonders what kind of a future awaits her in a time where nothing is certain and trouble lurks on every corner.

To find out more about *Finding Fortune*,
as well as discover other exciting books, visit:

www.catnippublishing.co.uk